AVENGER

AN OUTSIDER NOVEL
BOOK FOUR

MICALEA SMELTZER

DEDICATION

This one is for Caeden and Sophie.
Thank you for an incredible journey.

PROLOGUE.

I thought we had every reason to fight before.

But now, with the baby, fighting takes on a whole new meaning.

Fighting and winning, assures the baby's safety.

And I'll do *anything* to keep my baby safe.

Don't mess with a mama wolf.

ONE.

"We're having a baby," Caeden repeated softly under his breath. He looked up at me and his eyes shimmered with tears. "I'm going to be a dad." Caeden put his hand to my stomach, "There's really a baby in there?"

I giggled at his words. "Yes, there's really a baby in there."

"My baby," he whispered as his fingers caressed me through the thin fabric of my shirt.

"I'm going to be a grandma!" Both our moms exclaimed at the same time.

I looked at Caeden and laughed.

"Sweeeeet!" Bryce said, "I'm going to be the coolest Uncle in the history of Uncles!"

"You're not going anywhere near my kid," Caeden warned Bryce.

"Oh, come on!" Bryce threw his hands in the air. "Do you have to suck the fun out of everything?"

"When it involves my son or daughter, yeah."

Bryce rolled his eyes and looked at me. "I guess you'll have to play good cop with the kid. The poor baby isn't even here yet and Mr. Controlling is already dictating who the kid plays with."

I laughed. "That's probably because you'd drop the baby on its head," I joked.

"I would *never!*" Bryce feigned shock.

Amy chuckled and looked at her youngest son. "Well, there was that one time when you dropped Jake."

Charlotte smacked Bryce's arm. "You dropped my brother?"

"It was one time! One time! Why does everybody hold dumb stuff over my head!? I can be responsible…if I want to be."

The couch dipped down beside me and I looked over to see Gram. I gulped.

"A baby?" She looked at me, tears shimmering in her brown eyes.

I nodded, tearing up as well.

"I told y'all no babies for at least five years," her lower lip trembled. I don't think I had ever seen Gram so worked up before.

Caeden squeezed my hand. "I know, Gram, it just happened," I explained.

I expected a lengthy lecture on condoms and birth control, but she surprised me by wrapping her arms around me and rocking me back and forth.

"This is a blessing, Sophie. I know I said y'all should wait, and I meant that, but this will be the most loved baby on the planet. I'm going to shower it with gifts and love and kisses—I think I should move in!" She exclaimed, pulling away.

"I don't think so, Gram. Moving in won't be necessary. Caeden and I can handle this," I put my hand against my flat stomach.

It still hadn't sunk in yet that I was actually having a baby.

When I had missed my period I had chalked it up to everything going on with the pack, Travis getting away—yet again, and Logan dying. I had been under so much stress. But when it still didn't come, I knew. I don't know how, a mother's intuition maybe? Whatever it was, I was suddenly very aware that Caeden's child was growing inside me.

"You're so young," she said sadly, patting my cheek, "you haven't even lived yet."

"This is living, Gram," I smiled.

She patted my cheek and studied me. She shook her head and said, "It doesn't seem like you should be married with a baby on the way, Sophie. Just yesterday you were a little girl coming to visit me for the summer, begging for my cupcakes."

"I know," my voice cracked.

Suddenly, a sound like a honking horn filled the room. I turned in the direction of my dad, knowing that was the sound of him blowing his nose. "Dad?" I questioned.

"I'm fine," he said and his voice shook. "You're pregnant?"

Was I going to keep getting asked that question? I mean, come on people, I didn't know how much more blunt I could be.

"Yeah, dad, I'm really pregnant," I said quietly.

"My baby's having a baby," he cried and blew his nose again.

I had never, *ever*, in my eighteen years of life, seen my dad this emotional. My mom walked towards him and wrapped her arm around his shoulders. "He'll be fine," she mouthed at me before leading him from the family room.

I took a shaky breath and looked at the rest of the room. They all appeared to still be in shock.

Chris shook her head and seemed to come out of her stupor, letting out a high-pitched squeal that left my ears ringing. "You bitch! That's what you wouldn't tell me!"

"Guilty," I shrugged. Did she really think I'd tell her something like this before Caeden knew? She might have been my best friend, but Caeden deserved to know before everyone else.

"A baby! Do you know what this means?!" She cried.

"Uh—no?" I asked, a bit afraid of what her reply would be.

"Baby clothes and baby shoes! Aaaah!"

"Babe," Bentley pulled her against his side. "Calm down, and don't go getting any ideas," he chuckled.

"Oh please," she rolled her eyes, "I don't want a baby yet, even though we would have the cutest kid ever. Just look at us," she smirked, pointing at herself and Bentley.

Bentley shook his head, his lips quirking up at the corners as he fought a smile.

Nolan came over and sat down beside Caeden, clapping him on the shoulder. "Cay-berry, you must have some really powerful sperm."

"I'm leaving," Gram said, "when the topic of sperm gets brought up, my butt's outta here," she scurried from the room and towards the kitchen.

"I'll talk to you two in a bit," Amy said, following her.

"You really know how to clear a room," I told Nolan.

He shrugged. "I can't help it that people don't like it when bodily fluids get brought up. It's a fact of life."

"Amen," Bryce said. I was beginning to wonder if Nolan and Bryce were related...or at least from the same planet.

Caeden blushed and shook his head. "I—uh—actually I think I know when it happened..."

"What?" I snapped my head in his direction.

Rubbing his cheeks to hide the embarrassing redness, he coughed, "Um—in the shower, we didn't—"

My eyes widened as realization hit me. "Oh my god. You're right." I cradled my face in my hands, shaking my head. "We are so dumb."

"Dude," Bentley snickered, "always wrap it up."

"Shut up," Caeden glared at his best friend. He took one of my hands in his and used the other to cup my cheek. "I don't regret this, though. Believe that. I'm so incredibly *happy*. This is...amazing," he lowered his hand from my face and pressed it against my stomach, even now there was still awe on his face.

I knew we were young, newly married, and with the threat of Travis still looming over our heads, now certainly wasn't the best time for a baby, but like Caeden I was *happy*.

I hated to disturb Caeden, since he still had a hand pressed against my stomach, but I knew I really needed to find my dad.

"I'll be right back," I kissed his cheek as I stood.

It didn't take me long to find my mom and dad. They were sitting on the steps and my mom was talking to him in hushed tones.

"Dad?" I questioned hesitantly, wringing my hands together.

He looked up at me and although he wasn't crying anymore, his eyes were red-rimmed.

"Hey, baby girl," he swallowed thickly. "I'm sorry for how I acted. I'm just…really surprised."

"Well, I am married." I cringed at my own words. Bad joke.

He tried to smile but failed. "I know…but us dads like to pretend our daughters are completely innocent."

I closed my eyes and winced. "Can we *please* change the subject?"

My mom laughed, patted my dad on the shoulder, and said, "I'll leave you two alone to talk."

I watched her disappear into the kitchen and sat down on the stairs beside my dad.

"So…the kid isn't going to call me grandpa, right? I'm too young to be a grandpa," he bumped my shoulder.

"What do you want the baby to call you?" I asked, smiling.

"I don't know," he took a deep breath. "What about PapPap?"

"Whatever you want, daddy," I laughed, shaking my head. "You have about eight months to figure it out."

He stared at me for a moment and tears shimmered in his eyes once more. "You're not my little girl anymore. You're all grown up and that makes me sad. Don't get me wrong, I love Caeden, but I miss the days when I was your favorite guy."

"Dad," I laid my head on his shoulder, "you're still my favorite guy, you're just tied with someone else now. I have plenty of love for the both of you. No matter what, you're always going to be my dad. I might not be the little girl playing dress up and asking you to be my prince, but I am still Sophie."

"I know," he kissed the top of my head. "It's hard on us parents to accept the fact that our children have to grow up and become adults themselves. Now," he glanced at my stomach, "you're going to get to experience that."

"You know," I smiled, "I'm going to need a lot of advice. I've never even changed a diaper."

He chuckled. "You know this baby will be the most loved baby in the whole world. You have nothing to worry about, Soph. Between me, your mom, Gram, and Caeden's mom, this baby will be spoiled rotten."

"Do you think I can do this?" I hated voicing my concerns aloud, but I knew my dad was the only person who wouldn't judge me for my fears.

"I know so," he assured me. "You have nothing to worry about."

"Thanks, dad, I needed to hear that."

"Anytime," he stood, holding out a hand to pull me up. "Let's get this place cleaned up."

With everyone's help, we had the house clean in no time.

I hugged my mom, dad, and Gram close as I said goodbye.

Soon, it was just me, Caeden, and Nolan left.

Nolan leaned by the front door, eyeing us. "Um…I'm going to head out for a while. I'll see you two later," he chuckled and before either of us could reply he was opening the door and gone from our sight.

I shook my head at Nolan's strange behavior.

"I'm so tired," I told Caeden as I started up the steps.

"Maybe you should take a hot bath," he suggested as the dogs ran up beside us.

"Whoa," I started to lose my balance when Murphy's tail slammed into me.

Caeden's hand shot out to steady me and keep me from crashing to the ground. "Are you okay?" He asked, concern lacing his voice.

"Yeah, fine, just a bit dizzy," I put a hand to my forehead and continued up the rest of the steps.

"Sophie," he started, "we're shifters...we have excellent balance you shouldn't have fallen."

"I'm tired," I reasoned, opening our bedroom doors. Both dogs bound onto the bed.

"Still, that shouldn't have been a factor."

"What are you saying?" I turned to look at him with my hands on my hips.

"I don't know," he rubbed the back of his head. "Could the baby—"

I stopped him right there with a glare. "Don't start, Caeden. I mean it. I love you, I do, but don't you dare try to turn my pregnancy into an excuse to protect me from everything. I won't let you do it."

"I'm just concerned," he followed me into the bathroom as I started a tub of hot water, adding bubble bath.

"And I understand that," I turned around and took his face between my hands, "but you have to learn that you can't worry about everything, and you can't control me. I am my own person, Caeden."

"I know," he whispered.

"Then why is there still a wrinkle in your brow?"

"Because, you're my mate, Soph. It's my job to worry about you," he explained.

"Every job has a vacation, let it go," I kissed him.

"Nice try," he smirked when I pulled away.

"It was worth a shot," I laughed.

By the time I got in bed, I was exhausted and fell asleep as soon as my head hit the pillow. But sleep was short lived. It wasn't long until the nightmare consumed me...

My body slammed into the tree and I felt my insides breaking apart. The mutant stalked towards me and smiled triumphantly. This was it. He was going to kill me.

Just when I prepared to close my eyes, a wolf slammed into the mutant. The wolf took out the mutant's leg. When the wolf turned his head to check on me, the not quite dead mutant used that to his advantage. The mutant grabbed the wolf by the neck and twisted. It happened so fast—I counted two of my heartbeats and the wolf was dead.

Horrified, I stared into the dead green eyes of Logan.

This couldn't be happening. It was my fault he was dead. I would have to live with the knowledge that Logan died protecting me for the rest of my life.

I sat straight up, sobbing, my clothes drenched in sweat.

"Sophie?" Caeden sat up, rubbing his eyes. "What's wrong?"

"My fault," I gasped breathlessly. "It's my fault."

"What are you talking about?" His thick brows furrowed together in confusion.

"L-L-Logan is dead…because of me," I cried.

"Oh, Soph," Caeden took my face between his hands. "That's so not true."

"It is," I sobbed, letting him wrap me in his arms. My tears soaked his bare skin but he didn't seem to mind.

"We can't blame ourselves for things that are out of our control," his fingers tangled in my hair.

"If I hadn't got hurt—"

He pulled me away from his chest and pressed a finger against my lips. "But you did get hurt, Soph. Logan *saved* you, baby. He gave up his life so you could live yours, don't ruin his gift by dwelling on the past. What is, is."

"Aren't you sad he's gone?" I choked.

"God, of course I am. He's been my friend since we were little, even though we weren't close, he was still always there. I'll miss him for the rest of my life. But without his sacrifice, I wouldn't have my wife or my child," he swallowed thickly. "Missing him is one thing, but being angry and stuck in the past questioning everything is an entirely different thing." He brushed my hair behind my ear with a sweep on his warm fingers.

"I want to rip Travis apart for causing this," I growled, my fingernails digging into Caeden's skin.

"Shhh, my she-wolf," he whispered.

"What? You don't feel the same way?" I questioned, gazing up at him with wide eyes.

"Oh, I do," his eyes narrowed and his jaw clenched, "I plan on avenging the deaths of everyone in my pack. I can promise you, Travis will experience tenfold what he dished out. He won't know what's hit him."

TWO.

I stood in the kitchen, half asleep, and jumped when the orange juice I was pouring into a glass sloshed on my feet.

I jumped back, blinking blearily at the mess I had made. Orange juice pooled on the counter, dripping off the edge onto the floor. The tops of my feet were covered with the sticky substance and I knew if I went upstairs to wash my feet, I'd track through the house. So, I jumped up on the opposite counter and swung my feet into the stainless steel sink. I turned the water on warm and began to scrub the stickiness from my feet.

"Good—what the—?" Nolan stopped in the doorway of the kitchen looking at me like I'd grown three heads. "Is your shower broken or something? 'Cause you do know you're a little too big to bathe in the sink."

"I spilled orange juice everywhere," I explained with a sweep of my hand.

His eyes landed on the mess and he chucked. He crossed his arms over his muscular chest and eyed me. "And how does a shifter make a mess like that?"

"Tired," I grumbled.

He tilted his head, indicating that I needed to explain further. "Nightmares," I mumbled under my breath. Nolan was the last person I wanted to talk to about this. I didn't know him like Caeden did.

"Oh," he nodded. "I've been there."

"You have?" My head shot up.

"Mhmm," he nodded, striding further into the kitchen. He grabbed a rag and began to mop up the mess. He also took the time to toss a cloth at me to dry my feet.

"Mhmm? Is that all I get?"

"Life sucks and shit happens," he growled with his back to me. "Sometimes we can't escape the residual effects, no matter how far we might run."

I knew I wouldn't get anymore out of him after that. Nolan never talked about why he left. I knew it bugged Caeden, but since he was scared of Nolan running off again, he didn't push the topic.

"Thanks for helping me clean up," I smiled at him as I hopped off the counter.

"It's not a problem."

Before either of us could say anything, we heard Caeden call our names.

Nolan and I exchanged a look and hurried to Caeden's office.

"What is it?" Nolan asked.

"Has something happened?" I chimed in as my heart raced a mile a minute in my chest.

Caeden sat in the leather chair behind the desk with his head in his hands. "Sit." He commanded.

I had never seen Caeden sound so...official.

"What's going on?" I asked, feeling like I had been called into the principal's office.

He lowered his hands from his face and sighed. "The elders can't be trusted."

"But Gram—"

"Not even, Gram," he whispered. "Do I think she's the mole? Hell no. But she's around the elders too much to be trusted. I'm sorry, but that's the truth."

I was shocked. Not trust Gram? But she was my grandma!

"I think you're being ridiculous," I argued. "Gram would never betray the pack! If the other elders are a part of this, Gram must not know!" I knew there was no way Gram would betray us like that.

"I know that, Soph," Caeden's blue eyes rooted me to the spot. "But the less she knows of what we plan, the safer it is for her. If there is indeed a breach in the elders, like I believe there to be, then they'll pump her for information. I'm trying to protect her."

"Oh." I sat back, soaking in his words. He'd really thought this through.

"The only people we can trust, is each other," he pointed to the three of us, "Bentley, Chris, Bryce, Charlotte and our parents. I have to say though," Caeden looked at me sadly, "we need to be careful what we say to our parents, just in case it gets back to Gram or one of the other elders."

"This is a mess," I groaned, lowering my head into my hands. "I feel like we can't trust anybody."

"That's kind of the approach I'm going with," Caeden rubbed his stubbled jaw. "I know there will be casualties, but I want to keep them to a minimum. The less everyone except for the three of us knows the better." His eyes were tired and his shoulders sagged in defeat. Losing Logan, and other pack members, had taken a toll on him.

I looked over at Nolan, suddenly questioning whether or not we could trust him. I mean, he *had* just shown up at our doorstep years after he'd disappeared. I hated to feel like we couldn't trust anyone. That thought made me feel so lonely. You should be able to trust your friends and family, but we couldn't risk it again. I understood where Caeden was coming from. It didn't mean I had to be happy about it though.

* * *

Two weeks passed as Caeden kept himself shut up in his office pouring over anything that could help us kill Travis and his mutants. He barely ate or slept. To say I was worried about him was an understatement.

I stepped into his office and he was oblivious to my intrusion. I leaned over the chair he sat in and wrapped my arms around him. He startled at my touch, but then relaxed.

"Come to bed," I whispered. "You're exhausted, Caeden. Shifter or not, this isn't healthy behavior."

"I need to find *something*," he whispered.

"Find what? Can I help you?" I questioned. At this point, I was desperate to do whatever it took to make him leave his office.

"No," he shook his head. "I've read over these books hundreds of times," he pointed to the book in his lap and even more covering the floor, "there's nothing in them that's helpful."

"And yet, you keep reading them hoping for a different outcome?"

"Silly, I know," he laughed humorlessly.

I hated seeing him tear himself apart like this. I knew he was the Alpha, but we were a *pack* and we should be doing these things together.

"Let's go to bed," I reached for his hand and he placed his in my open palm, "and starting tomorrow we do this *together*."

He smiled a genuine smile. "Deal."

THREE.

"Do you think we can trust Nolan?" I drew random designs on Caeden's naked chest when I asked the question. I couldn't make myself look in his eyes. This was a question that had been haunting me since the conversation between the three of us in Caeden's office two weeks ago.

"I've had my...doubts," he admitted, his chest rising and falling heavily. "But yes, I do believe we can trust him. Maybe him more than anyone else."

"Why?" I questioned as the morning light began to stream through the windows.

"He's...Nolan. There would be no reason for him to betray us."

"Then why would the elders betray us?" I continued to trace my finger over his chest.

"Because they don't want me as Alpha," he whispered.

I sat up, my hair sweeping down and around my shoulders. "That makes no sense."

"Yes, it does," Caeden sat up too. "As soon as my dad died, they were determined to make sure I wouldn't become Alpha, but there was nothing they could do."

"Explain," I pleaded. Everyone always seemed to forget that I didn't grow up knowing I was a shifter. There were so many things I had no clue about.

"You see...if we have a son and something would happen to me, he wouldn't be able to take over the position of Alpha until he was seventeen and even then he'd have to go through trials to prove himself." He ran his fingers through his hair and continued, "In the meantime, someone else would be assigned as a temporary Alpha. Since I was seventeen when my dad was—*murdered*," he forced the word out, "there was nothing the elders could do, but give me the position." He swallowed thickly. "Luckily, since I was of age, they didn't put me through the trials. But they did think I was too...soft hearted for the position."

"What's wrong with that? The fact that you *care* is a good thing," I placed my hand over his heart, reveling in the steady thumping.

He placed his hand over mine. "They said it makes me weak and easily distracted."

"Who the hell are these elders?"

"They're composed of our grandparents," he tucked a piece of hair behind my ear.

"I thought your grandparents were dead or something? You never talk about them."

"My grandparents have all passed away. The elders are made up of what's left of our generation's grandparent's. It's Bentley's grandpa that hates me the most. He felt that Bentley's dad should have been Alpha instead of me."

"Wow," I breathed. "I've never quite understood the politics of this world."

"It sucks," he frowned. "I hate it, to be honest. I'm sick of the elders trying to control everything so much. Did you know, we're not allowed to be involved with humans and if they find out they'll kill you?"

"Oh my God," I gasped. "That's horrible!"

"I think that's why Nolan left," he mused.

"Because he fell in love with a human?" I questioned.

He nodded, looking at me between his long black lashes. "He was always a rebel," he fought a smile.

"Still, they'd kill him because he fell in love with a human? That's just...so wrong."

"Each shifter community has its own set of elders and they're all stuck in the past. It's like they've forgotten what it's like to be young," he mused.

"There's so much I don't know," I whispered sadly, rubbing a finger over his collarbone.

"You're better off not knowing, Soph," his fingers tangled in my hair and he forced me to look at him.

"It isn't fair for you to decide that for me," I frowned. "I'm your wife, Caeden, but I'm also an Alpha too. I *need* to know these things. Not knowing them makes me vulnerable, and I don't think you want that."

A wrinkle creased between his brows and I leaned forward to kiss it away.

"You're right," he breathed, kissing my neck. "You're always right."

"Of course. I'm brilliant," I laughed—one of the first *genuine* bouts of laughter I'd had since Logan died.

"I've missed that," Caeden reached to cup my cheek.

"What?"

"Your laugh...your smile," he brushed his thumb over my bottom lip. "I hate seeing you sad and not being able to do anything about it."

I frowned. "You do everything." And that was the truth. Caeden didn't realize how much he helped me by just being him. He was my rock. He kept me grounded and sane. Did I get mad at him? Sure. But I knew he'd always be there for me, we were mates after all. Caeden understood me, though, the good and bad parts.

"Hey," he said, snapping me out of my thoughts.

"What?" I blinked my eyes, trying to focus on what he was saying.

"Where'd you go? You kinda blanked out on me," he chuckled, tucking a piece of hair behind my ear.

"Sorry," I shook my head, gazing down at the sheets, "I was just thinking about us."

"Oh, really," he chuckled, nibbling on my chin.

"Mhmm," my eyes closed and I leaned towards him.

"Good things, I hope," he whispered huskily as his lips grazed my ear. Two minutes ago we'd been talking about the crappy elders and now all I could think about was losing myself in his love and warmth.

"Always," the word left my lips on a breathy sigh. He peppered kisses along my jaw and down my neck. "Caeden," I breathed, my fingers tangling in his wavy hair.

"Come here," he growled low in his throat, grabbing me around the waist and pulling me onto his lap. His lips covered mine and I let him take away all my fears and doubts with his touch.

* * *

"I love you," Caeden nuzzled my neck, pulling me against him.

"I love you too," I giggled, trying to pull out of his embrace, "but we really need to get dressed to get to the doctor's in time."

"I know," he kissed my lips and released me.

I returned to searching through the closet for something to wear.

"I can't believe we get to hear that baby's heart today," he smiled at me. "That seriously blows my mind."

I nodded in agreement. Hearing and seeing the baby would make it even more real. A part of me still couldn't believe that in a matter of months, we'd have a baby to hold. It blew my mind.

Unfortunately, I felt like I couldn't really enjoy my pregnancy. We had so much to worry about with Travis and the mutants. I wanted him dead before the baby came. No way was I having a baby with Travis still posing a threat. I'd rip him apart limb by limb—

"Sophie?" I shook my head as Caeden's voice interrupted my thoughts. "You okay?"

"Yeah," I forced a smile. "Just thinking about the baby."

His grunt told me he didn't believe me, but he decided not to pester me about it.

Pulling on a shirt, I turned to face him. "I meant what I said last night. We do this together. Let me help you."

"I know you meant it," he bent and kissed the top of my head. "And I understand where you're coming from. Locking myself in my office and reading The Legends over and over again, isn't going to solve anything. Two brains are better than one," he winked at me.

"Or three if you let Nolan help," I pointed out. "Even more if you asked our pack to help you."

"I'd prefer to keep them out of this…for now at least. I'm not quite ready to tell them my belief of the elders…especially Bentley. He may be my best friend, but blood is thicker than water and I don't want to push him away."

"I understand," I slipped on a pair of flip-flops. "You ready?"

"Yeah." Caeden was all smiles. "When do we find out if it's a boy or girl?"

"It's way too soon for that. Probably around Christmas," I shrugged.

He wrapped an arm around me and pulled me against his solid chest. "And what a wonderful Christmas present that will be."

"What would you prefer? Boy or girl?" I questioned curiously.

"I don't care, honestly. Either way, I'm the luckiest guy alive. I have a beautiful wife and a sweet little baby to look forward to."

I took his scruffy face between my hands and stared into his blue eyes. "Can you believe, this time last year we'd only just met?"

"It feels like I've known you forever," he murmured. "I don't know what I'd do without you."

"Same."

No other words needed to be spoken.

I breezed past him and bound down the steps into the kitchen. I opened the pantry and grabbed a box of cereal before grabbing a bowl and milk from the refrigerator.

"Morning."

I nearly jumped out of my skin. "Jesus! Why do you have to do that?" I glared at Nolan. He was reclined casually at the built-in breakfast nook chewing on an apple.

"It's fun to scare you," he smirked. "I've never been around a shifter that's so…human."

"It's annoying," I glared at him as I poured milk over my cereal.

"I find it amusing," he took another bite of his apple.

"What are you two arguing over?" Caeden asked, breezing into the kitchen.

"Nothing, Cay-berry," Nolan chuckled.

"Sure," Caeden drawled as he fixed himself his own bowl of cereal.

"Where are you two headed?" Nolan asked, spinning the apple core on the tabletop. "You look like you're on a mission and I'm not invited."

"Doctors appointment," Caeden answered, shoveling cereal into his mouth with one of the large wooden spoons you use for baking.

"We have regular spoons, you know," I commented, trying to contain my laughter.

"Oh, I know. But this is more efficient," he chuckled. When most of the cereal was gone, he brought the bowl up to his lips and tilted it back. His throat muscles flexed as he swallowed and I found myself having to look away. How did he manage to make everything he did seem so sexy? It really wasn't fair.

I finished my own bowl and emptied the milk in the sink before sticking the empty bowl in the dishwasher.

"I might not be here when you guys get back," Nolan muttered as he stood. He stretched his arms above his head and his thin t-shirt rode up a bit showing off his tanned and toned stomach. Before Caeden, I would have been attracted to Nolan. He was definitely a good-looking guy.

"Where are you going?" Caeden asked, his brows furrowing together.

"Out, Cay-berry, and that's all you need to know," Nolan clapped Caeden on the shoulder as he passed.

Caeden and I exchanged a look. "I'm sure it's fine," Caeden mouthed so Nolan wouldn't overhear.

I shrugged in reply, because I wasn't so sure.

* * *

"This is...*awkward*," Caeden's knee bounced nervously as he glanced around at all the pregnant women.

"You didn't have to come," I whispered in his ear.

He turned to glare at me. "Of course I did. This is my baby too. I *want* to be here. I've just never seen so many pregnant ladies in one place before," he chuckled.

"I'm one of those pregnant ladies," I poked his arm.

"Yeah, but you're not—you know—showing yet," he rolled his hands in front of his stomach.

"I'm going to show soon," I snapped. Oh no. Were these my pregnancy hormones already kicking in?

"And you'll be beautiful," he put a hand over my stomach, lovingly rubbing his fingers over the cotton of my shirt.

"Nice save," I muttered, wondering how much longer we'd have to wait. We'd already been here an hour and all I wanted was to see and hear my baby. It didn't seem like too much to ask for.

A nurse opened a door and stepped into the waiting room. Looking down at the clipboard, she asked, "Sophie Williams?"

"'Bout time," I muttered as I stood.

Caeden followed behind me, looking like a fish out of water. Poor guy.

"Right this way," the nurse directed.

My heart raced in my chest in excitement and fear. I had no idea what to expect. I hoped they didn't poke and prod me too much.

"Change into this," she handed me a gown. "The doctor will be in soon."

The heavy door closed behind her with a click.

"Well, this ought to be flattering," I stared at the nasty cotton gown she told me to put on. There was a divider so I went behind that to change. I knew Caeden had seen everything already, but I was scared someone might open the door and get an eyeful. I didn't need to deal with that embarrassment.

I tossed my clothes over the divider and called for Caeden. "Can you help me? I can't tie it."

"Sure," he came around the divider and quickly tied the hanging ribbons together.

I took a seat on the paper-covered bed thingy. I looked up at the bright halogen lights. "I feel like I'm about to be dissected or something."

Caeden chuckled as he sat down in the hard plastic chair once more. "I don't think that's going to happen," he scratched his stubbled jaw.

"How long do you think we'll have to wait?" I kicked my legs, looking around at the gross medical pictures depicting the joys of giving birth.

"Forever," Caeden pinched the bridge of his nose. "Before we shift, we get sick and injured like any other human, and I've spent countless hours waiting for doctors and it sucks."

"I can't wait to hear our baby's heartbeat," I whispered.

"Me too," he agreed, smiling so broadly that the dimple in his cheek winked at me.

A knock sounded on the door and then it cracked open.

"Hi, I'm Dr. James," the man said. "You must be, Sophie," he held a hand out to me.

"Yes," I took his hand and gave it a light shake, trying to hide my cringe. I remembered specifically asking for a female doctor. I didn't quite feel comfortable with some strange man I had never met before poking around down there. But I didn't want to cause a scene and delay seeing my baby any longer, so I kept my mouth shut.

"And you must be the husband," the doctor turned to Caeden.

"Yes, sir," they shook hands.

"So," Dr. James sat down on his chair, "how are you feeling, Sophie? Any morning sickness?"

"I haven't thrown up, but I have felt nauseous. I seem to be really dizzy. Is that normal?" I began to worry. I didn't want anything to be wrong, and I knew nothing about babies, let alone being pregnant.

"That's perfectly normal," the doctor assured me with a soft chuckle. "When it happens, just be sure to lay down and rest for a bit till it passes. We don't want you to get so dizzy that you fall."

I nodded in understanding.

"Any more questions?" He raised a brow, looking at me and then Caeden.

"When do we find out if it's a boy or girl?" Caeden asked.

I couldn't help smiling. He *really* wanted to know that.

"It's too early to tell that now. Once I get a good look at your baby and determine an approximate due date, I'll be able to let you know when a good time to schedule an appointment to find out the sex. As long as mom is okay with that?" Dr. James gaze swung my way.

"I want to know," I assured him, nervously fiddling with the scratchy hospital gown.

"Okay, good. I'm glad you're both on the same page. You have no idea how many couples can't agree on that. One wants to know, the other doesn't. It's exhausting. Some days I feel like I have to be a marriage counselor," he laughed, scooting his chair over the table and looking over a chart. After looking at it for a moment, he rubbed his hands together and said, "Let's see your baby."

* * *

Caeden couldn't stop smiling at the sonogram. "She's so tiny. She doesn't even look a baby," he said as we got in his Jeep.

"She?" I smiled.

A soft red hue inflamed his tanned cheeks. "Or he. But I think it's a girl."

"Why do you think it's a girl?" I pressed curiously.

He shrugged. "I don't know. I'd be happy with a boy, but I feel like we need more girls around."

"Well, I guess we'll find out…December twentieth," I looked down at the slip of paper with the appointment information for when we find out if we were having a boy or girl.

"I thought maybe we could meet our parents for lunch and show them this," he handed me the sonogram.

"Sounds good. I'll call them." I pulled my phone from my purse. Our parents were quick to agree and I picked a restaurant that would be easy for all of us to get to.

When I was finished with my phone calls, Caeden asked, "So…have you thought of any baby names?"

"Yes," I admitted, looking out the window. I already had plans for a nursery too, but I wasn't telling him that.

"What do you have in mind?" He asked.

"I don't want to say," I groaned, letting my hair fall forward to hide my face.

"Aw, Soph, don't be like that," he chuckled. "Tell me."

"If it's a girl…I was thinking Lucy…you know, a spin on Gram's name?"

"That would make Lucinda so happy," Caeden grinned, reaching for my hand as he drove. "What about for a boy?"

"I was thinking…we should name him Beau…I feel bad that my last name isn't being carried on since I don't have any brothers. I thought it would be a way to honor my dad and his middle name could be Roger to honor your dad."

Caeden was shaking his head and I thought for sure he was about to tell me that Beau was a horrible name. "Beaumont 'Beau' Williams…I love it, Sophie," he grinned. "As for Roger as a middle name…Bryce and I were talking the other day and he said that he wants to use the name Roger when he has a son. I don't mind, so I told him that was fine."

"That's sweet of you." I wanted to lean over and kiss him, but since he was driving I didn't think it was a very bright idea to distract him.

"Beau or Lucy," he repeated the names. "They're perfect. Honestly."

"I'm glad you like them," I smiled, pleased that he loved my choices. I should've known though, as mates we had a very similar thought process. Arguing wasn't typically part of our relationship...except recently with the whole Travis thing. I couldn't wait to be done with him and watch the light fade from his eyes—disturbing thoughts for a pregnant woman to have, but I'd be damned if I let Travis kill another pack member or do something to put my baby in jeopardy.

I had everything to fight for and everything to lose.

Travis had nothing.

So, in the end, who was the more dangerous one?

FOUR.

My dad cried when I handed him the sonogram. He was really going to have to stop doing that. This was getting embarrassing.

"Dad? Dad? *Daddy!* Please, we're in public. This isn't a bad thing. Can you please stop crying?" I begged. There was nothing wrong with a man crying, at least in my opinion, but when the man is your dad and he blubbers and blows his nose like a walrus *then* there is a problem.

"Sophie," Caeden rubbed my shoulder soothingly. "Let him cry. This is emotional for him."

"I'm sorry," my dad sobbed, hiding his face behind a napkin. "I'm happy. I swear. Just give me a minute."

I scooted out of the booth and went to hug my dad. He held me tight and didn't let go for several minutes. When he finally did release me, he'd stopped crying and managed to compose himself.

As I sat down, a waitress appeared to take our order.

"I'm going to be a grandpa!" My dad announced to the waitress.

She laughed. "I kinda figured that out."

I laughed in embarrassment, hiding my face as I gave her my order. We'd barely been here ten minutes and I was already close to bolting out the door. I wasn't sure how I'd get through this pregnancy with my family.

I was shocked by my dad's teary reactions to everything. I mean, once upon a time he *had* been Alpha. You'd think he'd be too…macho for this. But I was his only daughter, so I guessed his reaction was understandable…if a bit funny.

Our moms sat talking to each other and I glanced warily at Caeden. Why did I have a feeling that they were planning the baby's whole life?

"What is it?" Caeden asked when he noticed my expression.

I nodded my head to our moms sitting across from us. "They look like they're plotting something?" I hissed.

He chuckled, flicking his dark hair out of his eyes. "They're probably talking nursery decorations."

"*Great*," I sighed, taking a sip of water.

"Are you okay?" Caeden asked me, his brows furrowing together.

"Just tired, so naturally that makes me cranky," I frowned. I hadn't realized pregnancy would be so draining on my body. I wondered if that was normal or just a shifter thing. I felt so sluggish. I didn't like it.

Our food was brought out and we chatted as we ate. By the time we finished I couldn't wait to get home and take a nap. I marched straight up the steps and climbed beneath the covers. The dogs snuggled beside me and I was out like a light.

* * *

I sat up and looked around, rubbing at my eyes. The bedroom was dark and the clock on the table indicated that it was two in the morning, but I was wide-awake. I'd never awakened from my nap and now I was all messed up. Apparently I was becoming nocturnal.

I eased out of the bed, careful not to disturb Caeden or the sleeping dogs. I'd given up on trying to get them to sleep on the floor.

I tiptoed down the stairs and into the kitchen. I was *starving*.

I found some left over mac n' cheese and warmed it in the microwave. I grabbed a spoon and stirred it around before taking a bite. As I turned, my eyes connected with someone else's. Black soulless eyes. I knew those eyes and they only belonged to one person.

My heart raced in my chest and I struggled to breathe.

The bowl dropped from my hands and clattered to the floor. Pieces of macaroni flew everywhere.

I screamed like I was being murdered.

But he was there.

Right *freakin'* there.

And he was *laughing* at me.

I stormed forward, determined to get outside and sink my teeth in his flesh. I felt the telltale tremors shake my body as I began to transform.

"Sophie!" Caeden yelled and a light flicked on so the room was bright with light.

"Travis is right there," I pointed out the window. My hand lowered slowly. He was gone. "He was there, I swear!" Tears pricked my eyes.

Nolan came running into the kitchen and having heard what I said, told Caeden, "Stay with her, I'll check it out."

Caeden wrapped his arms around me as I sobbed into his t-shirt. His body was taut with tension and I knew he wished he was the one out there, but he also had a duty to me. Under normal circumstances, I would've told him I was fine and to leave me be. But I couldn't get the words to leave my lips and my arms only clutched him tighter.

Liar.

My eyes squished closed as I remembered Travis carving the word into my arm. He'd done it with silver so it never healed.

Every single day, I had to look at my arm and be reminded of everything Travis had done. Even if he was dead, he'd always haunt me, he'd made sure of that.

"Tell me what happened," Caeden commanded, pulling me back so he could look at my tear streaked face.

"I-I-I-came to get something to eat and when I t-t-turned I saw him, there," I pointed at the exact window. "How could he be here, Caeden?" I sniffled.

"I don't know," he frowned, a wrinkle marring his forehead. "This place is protected, he shouldn't be able to get in...unless..."

"Unless what?" I prompted.

"The elders," he growled through his teeth.

"Why would they tell him how to get past the gates?"

"Why would they give him a heads up that we were preparing to attack?" He countered. "Soph, if the elders are responsible for all of this, like I believe, then we have to be careful. They want me, *us*, dead," his hand lowered protectively over my stomach.

I closed my eyes, taking a deep breath. What had we done to deserve this?

Caeden guided me over to the breakfast table and I sat down. He stood guard, his arms crossed over his chest as he scanned the window for a sign of Travis or Nolan.

My heart had yet to slow down and I felt like throwing up. What if I hadn't come downstairs and spotted him? Would he have found a way into the house? Oh, God.

"Hey," Caeden knelt in front of me. "You okay?" His fingers tangled in my hair.

"No," I admitted.

His lips pressed tenderly to my forehead. "It'll be okay."

"Those words mean nothing when you can't say them with confidence," I countered.

"So maybe it won't be okay. But that doesn't mean that we stop trying to make things right."

I took a deep breath. Why did Caeden always have to be right?

Suddenly, Caeden stood up straight and his eyes scanned the yard relentlessly. "Nolan's coming back," he said unnecessarily.

The French doors opened and I forced my eyes away from a naked Nolan. Maybe one day—okay, probably never—I'd get used to all the nakedness.

"He was here, but he's gone now," Nolan panted breathlessly.

"Do you know how he got in?" Caeden asked.

"He climbed the fence."

"But," Caeden's eyes narrowed, "that's a high voltage fence. It may not kill a shifter, but it would definitely hurt like a bitch."

"It was disabled," Nolan answered.

Caeden cursed under his breath. He paced the length of the kitchen with his hands on his hips. His whole body was tense and I knew he was beyond angry.

"I'm sick of this!" He slammed a fist down on the island countertop. I jumped at the sound.

"Caeden," I said his name calmly and approached him slowly. I placed a hand on the bare skin of his back and the muscles jumped at my touch. "Just be glad I saw him."

"He could have gotten in the house, Sophie!" Caeden swung around and his face expressed just how livid he was. I hated seeing Caeden mad and worried all the time. I missed the carefree, goofy guy he was when I met him. But we had so much going on that I understood why he couldn't be that guy anymore—that didn't mean I had to be happy about it though.

"But he didn't," I reasoned.

My words didn't do anything to calm him. Out of the corner of my eye, I saw Nolan slip out of the room. Smart guy.

"I would never forgive myself if he hurt you or the baby," Caeden swallowed thickly and his blue eyes sparkled with fire. "I already let him get to you once. I won't let it happen again."

"Caeden," I groaned, "you have got to stop beating yourself up over that."

He shook his head, his jaw clenched. "It tears me apart to know that I can't protect you."

"Protect me? What about protecting yourself? Protecting the pack? *I'm* not the most important person in the world, Caeden. You have to stop worrying so much about me. If something happens to me, it does." I hated to be so morbid, especially with our child growing inside me, but the reality was that I could die. Or Caeden could die. It sucked to think about, but it was the truth.

"I refuse to accept that," he glared at me.

"If—God forbid—I would die, you have to let it *go*," I pleaded.

"I don't want to talk about this," he shook his head rapidly back and forth as he stared at the floor.

"We have to!" I screamed, trying to get him to listen to me. "We have to," I repeated in a softer tone.

His expression softened and he reached up to cup my cheeks between his hands. "I'm sorry," he leaned his forehead against mine. "But talking about death…that's not something I'm comfortable with. I refuse to think about the possibility of losing you or our baby. You're both," one of his hands lowered to press against my stomach, "the most important thing to me."

I understood where he was coming from. Did I want to think of the possibility of Caeden dying? Hell no. But it was something I had to accept might happen.

"We're going to kill Travis and his mutants," Caeden promised, "and all of this will have been nothing but a distant nightmare."

FIVE.

Unfortunately I didn't possess the same confidence Caeden did. Thus far, we'd been unable to kill Travis. There was no guarantee that we'd manage to kill him and the mutants this time. True, we'd greatly depleted his numbers when we fought the last time *but* he could easily make more mutants.

The stress of worrying about Travis and what the future may hold was really taking a toll on me. What if something happened to Caeden? I'd be left without my mate and our child wouldn't have a father. If something happened to me, Caeden could lose me *and* the baby.

I was beginning to wonder if it was worth it to go after Travis.

I stopped that thought as soon as I had it, because it was worth it. Logan deserved to have his death avenged. He died to save me and I wouldn't let his death have been in vain. I would squash Travis like a bug.

"Sophie?"

"Huh?" My head swung Caeden's way. After discovering Travis lurking outside, neither of us were able to go back to sleep and ended up going into his office to read through books and talk about things.

"Are you okay?"

"Yeah, sorry," I frowned, shaking my head. "I was just thinking about things," I mumbled.

Worry shimmered in his cerulean blue eyes.

"I'm fine," I said before he could comment. I wasn't in the mood to hear what he had to say. Empty promises were getting old. All I wanted was to have this over with and live a normal life...*a normal life*. I was a shifter, my life was never going to be normal by human standards, but I'd like for it to get to the point where there wasn't so much bloodshed. Was that too much to ask for?

"I'm not an idiot, Soph," he groaned, shoving the book he was reading off his lap. It thumped against the floor and I jumped at the sound. "Stop saying you're fine when I know that's not true. We're *mates*. Do you not understand what that means?" He looked at me fiercely. "I know when you're bothered by something. *Talk* to me. *Please*," he begged, reaching for my hands.

I sniffled, fighting tears. I turned away so he couldn't see my weakness, but it was useless. He reached up with one hand and took my chin between his fingers so that I was forced to look at him.

"I love you, Sophie. I'm your husband, you can talk to me about anything," he pleaded with me to open up.

I hated being seen as…weak and right now I was an emotional wreck. I was afraid if I opened my mouth I'd just start crying.

"Sophie, please," his thumb grazed over my bottom lip and a shudder racked my body.

"I just want this to be over," I admitted. "I want the fighting and the bloodshed to end. I want everything to go back to normal, Caeden. I don't want to bring our baby into this," my hand naturally fell to my stomach.

"I don't either," he brushed strands of my hair away from my eyes and tucked them behind my ear. "That's why I'm doing all this," he motioned to the books scattered all over the office. "It's why I'm not calling pack meetings. I need to get all this figured out in my head," he pointed to his forehead for emphasis, "before I say anything to anyone. I want to be one hundred percent ready this time. The next time I see Travis, I *will* kill him. My family—you and the baby—are the most important things to me. I won't let Travis take you from me."

I leaned into his touch, desperate to believe those words. But I wasn't the naïve girl I once was. I was a fighter now and I knew that words meant nothing. Promises held no backing. Caeden could tell me everything would be fine as much as he wanted, but that didn't make it true, no matter how much I might wish it so.

But I didn't tell him that. Instead, I closed my eyes and pretended that he was right. It was what he needed. I wasn't about to burst his bubble…at least not right now.

Caeden needed to believe that everything would be okay, so I'd give him that, because I loved him.

My phone started ringing and I pulled away from Caeden. I reached for my back pocket and looked at the name flashing across the screen. My brows furrowed together in confusion. I felt Caeden's curiosity as he stared at me. "It's Evan," I said. "I better take this."

I stood from the leather couch and walked across the office to gaze out the window for some semblance of privacy. "Hello?"

"Hey, Sophie, it's Evan," he said in a lazy drawl. Hearing his voice made me realize how much I had missed my human soccer-playing friends. With everything going on I couldn't remember the last time I saw them. I was a sucky friend.

"I know," I smiled, placing my palm against the window. "What do you need?"

"Well, I was just talking to Brody and we're sorry that we didn't get to see you before we left for Virginia Tech. I know it's a few months away, but do you think we can all get together over Thanksgiving break? I've already talked to all the other guys and we're all coming home. It can be sort of like a reunion," he rambled in typical Evan fashion.

I laughed, looking over my shoulder at a smiling Caeden as he eavesdropped on my conversation. "I'm sure we can work something out. I miss you guys."

"We miss our she-wolf!" I heard Brody yell in the background. I shook my head despite the fact that they couldn't see me.

"I'm really sorry I didn't see you guys before you left for college. I'm the suckiest friend ever," I frowned, feeling sad.

"You're busy," Evan replied. It sounded like something fell somewhere in their room. "Shit," Evan cursed, "I have to go."

"Bye," I said as he hung up.

Caeden was snickering behind me. "Those guys are highly entertaining."

"I think you're easily amused," I smiled easily, wrapping my arms around his neck and pressing my body into his.

"I lived with Bryce for too long, so yeah, I'm easily amused," he chuckled, kissing the end of my nose sweetly.

I was tall but I had to stand slightly on my tiptoes to kiss his lips. "I'm tired," I yawned, covering my mouth with my hand. "I'm going to go lay down for a while."

Caeden frowned, studying my face. "I don't like you being this tired, Soph."

I rolled my eyes at his worrisome nature. "I *did* lose a lot of sleep last night after spotting Travis. You should be sleepy too."

"I'm fine," he stated, "and you got more sleep than I did. Remember? You went to bed early."

"Caeden," I said his name in a scolding tone, "stop inventing stuff to worry about. I've been under a lot of stress. A nap won't kill me."

He watched me like I was a specimen under a microscope he was trying to decipher. "Alright, fine," he finally said, releasing his hold on me. I kissed his cheek and scurried out of the room before he decided to ask me a million questions about how I was feeling.

After everything I'd been through in the last year I had a right to be exhausted. Didn't I?

I climbed into bed and the dogs joined me. My eyes felt so heavy and my limbs felt weak. What if Caeden was right? What if this wasn't normal? Could something serious be wrong with me? Oh, God. I hoped not. Archie looked at me with wide brown eyes and they looked so sad. Did he know something to?

I took a deep breath. I couldn't let Caeden know his worrying was getting to me. After all, it was probably nothing.

* * *

When I woke from my nap I still felt *tired*. Like something was sucking all the energy out of me. I forced myself from beneath the warm covers. Maybe a nice hot shower would help. Yeah, that was it. That would ease the pulsing ache in my bones and make everything better.

I turned the water on as hot as I could stand it and stripped off my clothes. The water warmed my skin and I let it wet my hair so I could lather it with shampoo. With the scent of my coconut shampoo lingering in the air, I began to feel dizzy. I leaned heavily against the glass shower door, my fingers gliding across the wet glass. Something wasn't right.

I fell to my knees, pain zinging up my legs. Being a shifter, something like this shouldn't be happening in the first place, let alone hurting. My stomach heaved and I felt like I needed to throw up but nothing came out of my stomach. I curled into the fetal position, the water falling down on my naked body.

I tried to get up, but I couldn't get my limbs to move. I felt paralyzed.

"Caeden!" I called, sobbing. "Caeden!"

I heard Archie barking and scratching at the closed bathroom door.

My body heaved again as my stomach tried to empty.

The bathroom door burst open and through the steam fogging the shower door I saw Caeden's form run towards me. He pulled the door open and reached inside to turn the water off. Soap still clung to my body.

"Sophie," his voice cracked in fear.

"I can't move," my words were shaky as I shivered.

He grabbed a towel, swiftly drying my body before wrapping it around me as he pulled me into his arms. He was trying to be strong for me, but I saw the worry shimmering in his blue eyes. Something was wrong with me.

He carried me into the bedroom, laying me on the bed. He was frazzled and not thinking straight.

"C-c-clothes," my teeth chattered together as my whole body shook.

"Right," he ran over to the dresser and returned with underwear, sweatpants, and a long sleeved shirt, despite the fact that it was September and such clothes should be unacceptable.

I was so weak that he was forced to dress me. I felt humiliated. No one wants to be unable to even dress themselves.

Once I was dressed he sat me up in bed. "I'm worried about you," he brushed my wet hair from eyes. I opened my mouth to reply, but he cut me off. "Don't even think about telling me you're fine," he growled. "That," he thrust a finger in the direction of the bathroom, "was *not* normal. Something's going on with you."

"I wasn't going to say that," I whispered. "I was going to say that you were right. Something has to be wrong with me, Caeden. I'm so weak and the dizziness is getting worse."

He sat there, holding me in his arms, staring off into space as he thought. Suddenly, he stood, cradling me in his arms like a small child. He tucked me under the covers and propped the pillows up behind me so that I was sitting up. He turned the TV on and handed me the remote.

"I'll be right back," he mumbled, leaving the room.

As soon as he was gone, I raised my shirt up, looking at my still flat stomach. "Please be okay, baby. *Please.* Mommy loves you," I begged as tears fell from my eyes. If something happened to my baby I'd never forgive myself.

43

Caeden returned a few minutes later with a glass of orange juice and a plate with buttered toast on it. "This should help…some," he handed the plate to me and set the glass on the table. He was pale and the worry still hadn't left his eyes. "I called Lucinda," he stated with his hands on his hips. He was looking around the room, avoiding my eyes.

"And?" I prompted.

"She's on her way over. It will probably take her about an hour to get here," his eyes finally landed on me and he studied my face carefully.

"Sit with me, please," I patted the empty space in the bed beside me.

He hesitated for only a second before sitting down.

"Will you hold me?" I asked hesitantly.

Without saying anything, he enfolded me in his arms. I inhaled his woodsy scent with a slight citrus tang. It was the best smell in the world, because it reminded me of home. That's what Caeden was to me—not just my husband and mate, but my home.

I clung to his shirt with weak fingers. Neither of us said anything more, not wanting to spout false promises.

When Gram arrived, Caeden left me to let her in the house. I chewed my lip nervously. I hoped Gram knew what was wrong with me…but what if it was something really bad. Did I really want to know?

Gram entered the bedroom and stopped in the doorway. She looked as worried as Caeden. "Hey, sweetie," she said in a falsely sweet tone, trying to hide her worry. "How are you feeling?"

"Tired and dizzy." If I had to tell one more person that same thing I'd find a way to give them a swift kick in the knees.

She strode forward and began looking over me like a doctor would their patient. She asked me a million and one questions, checked my pulse, looked down my throat, and a bunch of other things.

Finally, she looked from me to Caeden. "I've never seen this before, but I've heard of it."

"What is it?" Caeden asked quickly. "Whatever it is we need to do to fix it, we will."

"There's nothing you can do to fix this," she shrugged and Caeden's eyes threatened to bug out of his head at her words. "It's the baby."

"The baby?" Caeden and I asked simultaneously.

She nodded. "This is rare...but it's possible when both the father and mother come from a strong Alpha line...basically, the baby is very strong and growing stronger every day. It's draining you, Sophie."

"Draining her?! Like a parasite!" Caeden exclaimed, backing away.

"Our baby is not a parasite!" I yelled. "How dare you say that!" I seethed.

He paled as my words hit him. "I didn't mean it like that—"

"This pregnancy is going to be hard on you, Sophie," Gram continued like Caeden and I hadn't just been bickering. "I've never seen this happen firsthand, but you'll probably lose the ability to shift."

"What?! No!" I cried, trying to wriggle free of the covers. I felt like the blankets were suffocating me. "This *can't* be happening! I *need* to shift! We have to kill Travis before the baby comes!" I couldn't bear the thought of bringing my sweet innocent little baby into a world where a monster like Travis existed.

Gram pushed my shoulders back so that I couldn't get out of bed. "Shh," she hushed me. "Don't get yourself worked up, it isn't good for you or the baby."

I immediately shut up. Despite the threat of Travis, the baby was the most important thing to me.

"Good girl," Gram smiled. Turning to Caeden, she said, "She'll be bed ridden most of the pregnancy...if she's this weak this early into the pregnancy it's only going to get a lot worse. I hope you're ready to play man nurse," she patted Caeden's cheek. She hugged me goodbye and said, "Take care of my girl," to Caeden before she left.

"I can't believe she's causing this," Caeden frowned, stepping forward to place his hand on my stomach.

I put my hand over his, marveling at the fact that my little family was right here. "She's worth it," I said, even though I wasn't as convinced as Caeden was on the baby's gender.

"Everything will be okay," he pressed his lips to my forehead. I closed my eyes, soaking in his words. I needed to hear them, but I knew he had said them more for his benefit than mine. "I'll keep you safe."

SIX.

Day three of my purgatory or "bed rest" as most would call it, had me wanting to claw at my husband's face.

"*Caeden*," I whined. "*Please*, let me do something! I can at least read one of those while I lay here!" I reached for one of the many books piled on the bed that he was leafing through.

"No," he smacked my hand away with a light swat.

"I don't think reading is going to make me pass out from exhaustion," I pouted. "I need to do something or I'm going to go crazy trapped in this bed for nine months, which I'm not going to allow to begin with."

"Stop being dramatic, Soph," he chuckled, flipping one of the ancient pages in the book he was reading. "Holy crap! This is it! This is what I've been looking for!" The bed bounced with his excitement. I leaned towards him curiously, trying to peer at the yellowed pages.

"What is it?"

With a finger, he pointed to the page and read aloud, "The abominations known as mutants can only be created by those who have relinquished their humanity. An army of these abominations would make the one who created them—"

He paused and his eyes widened.

"What? It would make them—?" I prompted.

"Invincible." He swallowed thickly. "It would make them nearly invincible." He ran his fingers roughly through his wavy brown hair. "We don't stand a chance, Sophie."

"Don't say that," I begged.

"Don't you see? Travis is making an *army*," his arms fell to his sides. "I don't care how strong of a pack we are. We don't stand a chance against an army of mutants *and* Travis."

Dread filled my stomach. Had we always been doomed from the start to die?

47

"Look at this," he reached over and grabbed several newspapers off the bedside table, throwing them onto my lap. "Read the headlines."

I glanced at him before letting my gaze drop.

Each headline was much the same.

A human missing, presumed dead. Several mentioned decapitated bodies being found.

The police believe these disappearances and murders are the work of a serial killer. They have no other information to release at this time.

My hand came up to cover my open mouth.

"Oh my God," I gasped before leaning over and throwing up on the floor. I couldn't stomach the thought of so many innocent humans dying or being turned into mutants because Travis—and maybe the elders—wanted us dead.

Caeden pulled my hair back into a ponytail and held it as I was violently sick. When I finished, he eased from the bed to clean up the mess.

"I'll get you some juice," he said as he left the room.

"And let me brush my teeth," I pleaded, knowing he could hear me.

Tears streamed out of my eyes as I silently cried for all the people Travis had killed. No one deserved to die like that, and the only reason he was doing this was because of us. If I had never come here, maybe none of this would've happened. True, I wouldn't have Caeden or the friends I'd made, but I'd rather lose them then be responsible for so many innocent lives.

There had to have been at least eight newspapers there, and who knew how many articles I had missed. I was eighteen, I didn't read the newspaper, but Caeden obviously did.

When he entered the room he had a glass of water and orange juice—I had been craving orange juice like crazy. Without saying anything he went to the bathroom and came back with my toothbrush and toothpaste. Using the glass of water, I brushed my teeth. When I finished I looked up at a bleary-eyed Caeden. "How many?"

"Huh?" He asked, taking the glass of water and emptying in the bathroom.

"How many deaths?" I clarified.

He stopped at the end of the bed, his hands grasping the wrought iron in a white-knuckle grip. "Twenty six."

"And how many are still missing?" I let my eyes drop to the blanket covering me. I couldn't look at him right now.

"Soph—"

"Tell me," I hissed through gritted teeth. "I need to know."

"At least fifty, but Travis is crafty so I'm sure there are people missing that no one's even realized is gone. That being said, I'd guess closer to eighty."

"Eighty," I gasped, forcing the word out of my mouth. I felt like I was going to be sick again. My head fell forward into my hands. "No," I said. "No, no, no," I kept repeating the word, like as if by sheer will power I could change what he had said. "This has to *stop*," I growled.

"I agree," Caeden spoke. "But like I've told you, I'm not going into this blind anymore...not that we did before, but you know what I mean. When we're ready to attack, I don't want there to be any chance that Travis gets away. I want his heart ripped out and his blood on my hands."

I looked up at Caeden. We'd both changed so much in the last year. Neither of us were naïve children anymore. We'd learned love and loss—two things that changes a person forever.

Caeden straightened. "I have some things I need to do. Christian is coming over to sit with you."

"I don't need a babysitter," I rolled my eyes.

"Yes, you do," he forced a chuckle. "Besides, she misses you. Don't you miss her?"

"Of course," I shrugged, evading a real answer. I *did* miss Chris. I considered her my best friend, but after what happened with Logan—her brother dying to save me—I didn't quite know how to act around her. I knew it was wrong of me to avoid her, although, was it considered avoiding when you were trapped in bed?

"Where are you going?" I asked him.

"Out."

"That's vague," I glared at him. "You can tell me."

"It was meant to be vague," he rubbed his stubbled jaw.

"Ugh," I groaned. I didn't want to act like a fussy child, but I really thought we had gotten passed this whole 'keep Sophie in the dark' thing. I mean, really. "Come on, Caeden. Tell me."

"No," he said sternly.

"You need to tell me things," I exclaimed. "You said you weren't going to keep me in the dark anymore!"

"Fine!" He yelled. "I'm going to my dad's grave! With everything that's been going on, I missed the anniversary of his death! Okay?!"

"Oh." I felt like a complete and total bitch. "I can go with you, if—"

"No," he cut me off. His eyes and voice softened and he released his hold on the bed. "This is something I need to do by myself. Besides, you're not fit to get out of bed."

"I'm feeling stronger," I frowned. "I *do* need to get up and move some. Sitting in bed all day every day isn't good for me and the baby either."

"You showered today," he grinned.

"I don't think it counts since you made me sit on the bench and *you* did the washing part."

"At least you're clean," he winked.

It amazed me how one minute we could be arguing and the next we were cracking jokes. I guess that was the power of being mates.

"Am I interrupting something?"

We looked over to see Chris standing in the doorway. I hadn't even heard her enter the house. This pregnancy had zapped my shifter senses.

"Not at all," Caeden smiled. He walked to my side and placed a light kiss on my lips. "I'll be back soon."

When he was gone, I looked up to see Chris still standing awkwardly in the doorway. Her blonde hair had grown a bit longer since Caeden's birthday, but it wasn't as shiny and bouncy as normal. Her light green eyes weren't as happy as they once were, but there was still a naughty glimmer in them that no amount of heartache could ever steal from her.

"Hey."

"Hi," she forced a smile.

"Are you going to stand there the whole time he's gone?" I asked.

"No," a ghost of a smile lifted her lips. I patted the empty space beside me and she sat down awkwardly beside me.

"Here," I handed her the remote, "I'll even let you watch one of those annoying reality shows you seem to love."

"Thanks," she took the remote but didn't change the channel.

I wasn't one to force a conversation so I grew quiet, waiting for her to say something.

A little over an hour had passed when she turned the TV off and looked at me.

"I'm sorry."

"You're sorry?" My brows furrowed together. "For what? You haven't done anything."

"I got married."

I choked on my own saliva. "What did you say? I don't think I heard you right."

"You did," she held her hand out, showing me the intricate gold band that glimmered there. "After losing Logan, and knowing what we're facing, Bentley and I decided that we didn't want to wait."

"I-I-I—" I didn't know what to say. "Did you have a wedding?"

"No," she shook her head. "If we had a wedding, I wouldn't have been able to keep it a secret. I'd want you to be my maid of honor. I know things feel…awkward between us. But I don't want it to be that way. Logan dying wasn't your fault. I don't blame you, but I feel like you think I do."

My lower lip trembled with the threat of tears. "But it was my fault."

"Aw, Sophie," Chris pulled me into her arms, stroking my hair. My tears stained her shirt as I sniffled. She shouldn't have been the one comforting me. I was the reason her brother was dead.

I couldn't stop the tears though. And I didn't push her away.

* * *

Caeden

I stood in front of the grave with my hands shoved into the pockets of my shorts. This was the first time I'd been here since we buried my dad over a year ago. I hated being here. It made the fact that he was really dead and gone even more real. When I didn't have to stare at his grave, I could pretend that he was just gone an extended trip and he'd be back soon. But death is one vacation you never return from.

"Hey, dad," I mumbled, toeing the ground with my sneaker. "This is weird…talking to you like this doesn't seem right…you know, since you can't answer back."

I tilted my head back, cracking my neck as I looked up at the clear blue sky.

"I felt like I should visit you though…I know mom and Bryce came to see you. And I didn't. I'm sorry for that."

I swallowed thickly, looking around the empty shifter cemetery. The elders kept the place looking nice, the grass was mowed and flowers grew in abundance. The cemetery was located in the middle of the forest, near the elder's headquarters. It was exactly like a human cemetery, but we chose to bury our dead here and not with other humans.

"A lot has happened since you left us, dad. I met my mate. Her name is Sophie and she's the most gorgeous woman I've ever seen," I smiled, running my fingers through my hair. "We're having a baby. I'm going to be a dad...that really blows my mind."

I sat down on the grassy ground and stared at the headstone.

"Any advice for me?"

Of course he didn't answer. I wished he would though. I had no clue what I was doing. Being an Alpha, a husband, and now a father...it was all a bit much. My dad had been amazing father to Bryce and I, as well as an exceptional Alpha. He wasn't groomed to be an Alpha, but when his best friend, Sophie's dad, left the position to him, he never looked back. Everyone respected him. He could be tough when he needed to be, but at the end of the day he had *heart*. I knew I wasn't as good of a leader as my dad had been, but I was trying. I hoped I made him proud, wherever he was.

I picked up a blade of grass and twisted it between my fingers.

"I miss you," I admitted, plucking up more grass and getting more dirt under my fingernails.

I sat there for a while longer, before I stood and headed back to my Jeep.

I wasn't ready to go back home—I knew that was wrong of me, but it was true. Reading book after book, hoping for *some* information was getting exhausting. Plus, I was worried sick about Sophie and the baby. I was trying to hide my worry from her, but I knew Sophie saw through my façade. She had always been way to perceptive. It was one of the many reasons I loved her.

I started up the Jeep, following the dirt road back out to civilization.

Since I wasn't ready to go home, I headed to my mom's house.

"Bryce?" She called out when the front door opened.

"No, it's me," I replied, heading into the kitchen. The scent of homemade fried chicken filled the air, making my stomach rumble.

She turned away from the counter and a big smile spread across her face when she saw me. "Are you here for dinner?"

"I wasn't planning on it but," I sniffed the air, "I'm reconsidering."

"I hope you stay," she turned back to the counter and continued battering the chicken. "Where's Sophie?"

"Home," I shrugged.

She glanced at me over her shoulder and her brows raised. "I don't remember the last time you two have ever been without the other."

"Ha, ha, ha," I leaned against the doorway, crossing my arms over my chest. "She's on bed rest."

"Bed rest?" She washed her hands, wiping them on a towel as she faced me.

"Yeah," I shrugged, pushing my hair out of my eyes. I really needed to get it cut, but since getting my haircut was my least favorite thing ever, I avoided it at all costs. "Apparently since I'm an Alpha, and Sophie's an Alpha, it can make the baby really strong. Basically, she's draining Sophie. Lucinda said Soph might lose the ability to shift."

"She? The baby's a girl? I didn't know you could find out the gender this soon."

"Well, we don't actually know," I admitted. "I just think it's a girl."

"What if it's a boy?" She smiled.

"I'll still be happy. But it's a girl. I know it."

She laughed at me. "So, if you're not here to eat, why are you here?"

"I needed to get away for a while," I scratched my chin.

She frowned. "Want to talk about it?"

I squirmed. I was a guy, I never really talked to my mom about anything. *But* it was pack business that had gotten under my skin, so I should have been able to talk to her. But I was too scared about the possibility of a mole that I just shook my head. I'd never thought I would keep secrets like this from my mom. Thanks to Travis, I trusted no one. Except Sophie. Despite what I told her, I didn't trust Nolan. I was testing him, trying to find loose strands to his story. So far though, he was solid. I just couldn't figure out if he really returned because we heard we were in trouble. From the time we were boys, Nolan had always been secretive, and he was my friend and I wanted to trust him, but he had to earn it first.

"Not really," I finally answered after the lengthy pause.

"You know I'm always here for you," she smiled, her eyes crinkling at the corners.

"I know," I straightened, backing out of the kitchen. "I'm going down to the basement."

"Will you stay for dinner?"

"Maybe," I shrugged.

"If you don't I'll package up some food for you to take home."

"Thanks," I said as I headed down the hallway. I opened the basement door and my feet thumped against the steps as I stomped down them.

I flicked the light on and the space illuminated. I grabbed a pair of mesh shorts and changed so I didn't get my regular clothes all sweaty. I chose to forgo a shirt, knowing I would only drench it in sweat. I needed to work off some of my anger and confusion. For me, exercise was the best way to do that.

I got on the treadmill, forgoing a warm up since I didn't need it, and ran at a full sprint. I could feel my muscles flexing and pulsing with the movement. Sweat dotted my skin, but I didn't stop. I was running nowhere but in the process I was releasing my demons. I might never be okay again, losing my dad, nearly losing Sophie, and then having my pack members die had taken its toll on me. Maybe the elders were right and I was too 'sensitive' for this position. I felt like the weight of the world was on my shoulders and my knees were buckling under the pressure.

"Dude, slow the fuck down."

"Watch your language," I warned Bryce in a fatherly tone.

He came around the front of the treadmill and rolled his eyes dramatically. "Are your little virgin ears so sensitive to bad words that I must filter myself?"

"Words like that are disrespectful," I panted.

"It's just a word," Bryce reasoned. "Saying it's *bad* makes it bad."

"What do you want?"

"Nothing. Mom told me to come down here and check on you. She said you were acting weird," he picked at invisible dirt under his nails.

"I'm not acting weird."

"That's what mom said," he raised his hands in surrender. "Want to spar?"

"Sure," I answered, slowing the speed of the treadmill. Just before it came to a complete stop I hopped off.

We headed over to the mats and it was nice to have my mind only focused on the technicalities of sparring and not on anything else.

It felt good to release all this tension. Bryce didn't say anything as I fought him harder than normal. Even he knew I needed this.

I threw a particularly brutal punch towards his face and his arm shot up to block it. Our heavy breaths filled the air, echoing around the basement. I got through his defenses and my fist slammed into his stomach. Anger flashed in Bryce's eyes and he fought harder. Punch after punch, I let the pain consume me so I didn't have to think about anything else.

Spent, we both fell onto the mat, looking up at the ceiling. Neither of us could catch our breath.

"Better?" Bryce asked after a moment.

"Much."

"Boys?!" Mom opened the basement door and called down to us. "Have you killed each other?"

"Hardly," Bryce answered.

"Caeden, I really hope you'll consider staying for dinner," my mom said, making me feel guilty. I needed to get back to Sophie, but it had been a while since I'd had a meal made by my mom. I would take Soph some leftovers so I didn't feel too guilty.

"Sure, why not?" I sat up, draping my arms over my legs.

Bryce wrinkled his nose and stood up, staring down at me. "If you're staying for dinner, you better shower, you stink."

"Thanks, Bryce," I chuckled.

"Just tellin' you like it is," he shrugged, taking his shirt off and rubbing his sweat off with it. "Not everyone can sweat and still smell this delicious," he dropped his shirt on my face so I got a whiff of his body odor. That kid was never growing up, but I loved him anyway.

I threw his shirt at his back and he chuckled as he started up the steps.

Since the clothes I had been wearing were down here, I opted to use the shower here as well instead of going upstairs to what had once been my bedroom.

When I was showered and dressed, I jogged up the steps and into the kitchen. Mom already had the table set and my stomach rumbled.

"I'm glad you decided to stay," she stood on her tiptoes to kiss my cheek. "I've missed you."

Ugh, moms always knew how to make you feel guilty. I knew it had to be hard on her with me being gone. Dad wasn't around, obviously, and Bryce was with Charlotte all the time. *I'd* hate being in this big old house by myself, so I knew she had to be feeling the effects.

"I've missed you too, mom," I sat down at the table.

Bryce sauntered into the room like he was king of the world. "Where's my dinner, woman?"

"The table," my mom pointed, "where it always is, every single night."

"I think Bryce is part alien," I chuckled, tipping the chair I was sitting in back on two legs.

"He's something else," my mom shook her head, grabbing a glass of water and taking her seat.

"Alien standing right here, people," Bryce pointed to himself, pulling out his chair. "Although, I think I'm okay being called an alien. Aliens are cool…if I'm an alien does that mean I get to probe people?"

My mom spat out her water all over the table. "Bryce!"

"What did I say?" Bryce asked innocently.

"Sometimes I wonder who raised you," my mom wiped up the mess with a napkin.

"Wolves, mom. Wolves raised me," Bryce said in a deadpan tone.

"You're such a smart ass," I snickered.

"Language, Caeden," Bryce mimed my tone from earlier.

"Boys!" My mom yelled before we could argue further. I swear, she had to be more of a referee than a mom with us.

"This is delicious, by the way," I chose to change the subject as I devoured the homemade fried chicken.

"It's been a while since I made fried chicken, but I was cleaning the kitchen the other day and came across the recipe. I decided to give it a try to see if I could still make it."

"You definitely succeeded," I started on my third piece. "Mind if I take some back to Sophie?"

"Not at all. I actually already have some set aside," she nodded towards the counter.

I stayed to help clean the dishes and then grabbed the food to take home. I cursed when I started my Jeep and saw the time. Christian was so going to kill me—not to mention Sophie.

I parked in the garage and hurried inside.

"Where have you been?" Nolan asked when I entered the house.

"How's that any of your business?" I growled.

"So testy, Cay-berry," he raised his hands in surrender as I passed him. I certainly wasn't giving him an answer to where I'd been. He didn't deserve one. He was always sneaking off and not telling me where he was going, so why should I tell him?

I made it to the master bedroom and opened the door to find a giggling Christian and Sophie. Christian had Sophie's feet in her lap was painting the nails a pale pink.

"Caeden," Sophie gasped, looking over to see me standing in the doorway. "Are you okay? You were gone a while."

"I'm perfect now," I stepped forward, placing a light kiss on her lips. I had been desperate to get away, but now, I wanted nothing more than to be right here with Sophie. I'd never thought I'd find the love of my life, but I did, and thank God for that.

59

SEVEN.
Sophie

I woke before Caeden, a rarity these days. I rolled to my side, studying the planes of his face. The lids of his closed eyes flickered and I wondered what he was dreaming about. I reached out, unable to stop myself, and traced my fingers over his lips. He let out a moan and my insides squirmed.

His eyes opened slowly and he turned to look at me. "Mornin'," he smiled crookedly.

I propped my head up on my hand. "I love you. You know that, right?"

"Of course I know," he reached up and cupped my cheek.

"I almost lost you on this very day a year ago," I whispered sadly.

His eyes closed and he swallowed thickly as he remembered showing up at Gram's on Halloween injured from Peter Grimm.

"I thought I was going to lose you before I even had you," I admitted.

"Aw, Soph," he gathered me into his arms. "I'm here and I'm not going anywhere."

"But you could have."

"And so could you. I thought for sure Peter and Travis were going to kill you when you were kidnapped. I worried myself sick. It was the worst feeling in the world—thinking you were going to die and there was nothing I could do." He kissed my forehead and inhaled my scent. Changing the subject, he said, "You have no idea how much I love waking up to the scent of cookies. You're like my very own dessert."

"Hardly," I rolled my eyes. "So...since it's Halloween and we live in the middle of nowhere, that means no kids trick or treating. But I want to do something."

60

"I already decorated the yard and the house, what more do you want?" He smiled.

"I want to carve pumpkins and one for the baby," my hand ventured down to the small bump my stomach had become. Most people probably couldn't tell I was pregnant, the bump was so small, but I knew my baby was carefully nestled inside me and it gave me peace.

"Pumpkins? But it's so messy," he wrinkled his nose in distaste.

"I want to. *Please?*" I begged. Technically I wasn't on bed rest anymore, but I had to limit my activities. The simplest things made me exhausted. I had left the house a few times, but since each time resulted in me sleeping for twenty-four hours so Caeden wouldn't let me leave anymore—except for doctors appointments. But surely I could sit and carve a pumpkin.

He sighed and I knew he was caving.

"Please? I want to carve a pumpkin for the baby," my fingers grazed back and forth over his chest.

"Fine," he relented and I smiled triumphantly. "But you're not going with me to get them. You can stay with Nolan."

"I'm okay with that," I said quickly. I knew there was no point in arguing about going to pick my pumpkin, because Caeden would never let me, and I was sorta sick of sleeping for a day when I went out.

He chuckled. "I didn't know you could be so…agreeable."

"Yeah, well, sacrifices must be made. And as much as I'd like to go out and do things, I know staying home and limiting my activity is best for the baby."

Caeden leaned over and placed a light kiss on my lips. "I'll shower and head out. I won't be gone long. I don't like being away from my princesses."

"The baby could be a boy," I replied, just like I did almost every time he referred to the baby as a girl.

"Fifty fifty, baby, and I'm betting on a girl."

"Oh, so this is a bet now is it?" I laughed.

He stood and stretched his arms above his head. "Sure. If it's a girl I...never mind, I only see this blowing up in my face," he grinned crookedly.

"Afraid I'd win the bet?" I asked, raising a brow.

"Maybe," he smiled as he backed towards the bathroom door.

I shook my head and slowly eased from the bed. I felt like I did everything in slow motion nowadays. I didn't like it. And like Gram had warned, I'd lost my ability to shift...well, let's put it this way—I hadn't *tried* to shift, because my wolf side was silent. I *knew* it was gone and I was so weak anyway that I didn't see the point of testing it.

I slipped my feet into a pair of slippers and grabbed a light gray sweater to wrap around me. I was freezing all the time now—strange since I was a shifter and we tended to have a higher than normal temperature.

I slowly made my way down the steps, gripping the railing tightly in my hands for fear I'd get dizzy and slip.

I shuffled my feet along the floors and stepped into the kitchen. I was surprised to find it empty. Nolan seemed to spend most of his time in there eating everything he could get his hands on.

I decided to take the time to make Caeden and myself an egg sandwich. Lately, unless Caeden made my meal, I'd been living off of cereal or anything that was easy to make. I didn't like feeling so weak and tired all the time. Laying in the bed all the time was so not as fun as it sounded.

When the sandwiches were done I carried the plates over to the table and went back for two glasses of orange juice.

By the time I sat down and took the first bite of my sandwich, Caeden walked in, rubbing his damp curls.

"You made me breakfast," he smiled when he saw the plate.

I shrugged. "You've been doing so much for me, the least I could do is make you a sandwich."

He bent down and kissed my cheek before sitting across from me. "This is really good," he commented. "But you certainly didn't have to do this."

I laughed. "I'm certainly not as good of a cook as your mom."

He shrugged. "My mom has had to cook all the time, raising two hungry shifter boys and all their friends, so practice makes perfect."

I bit my lip, absorbing his words. In seven months, we'd have our own child, and it was only a matter of time before the others started popping out kids. Somehow, over night, we'd become adults. It still hadn't quite hit me that my childhood was gone. After all, I was only eighteen and that was young. But Caeden and I had the weight of the world on our shoulders—or so it seemed—and that made us seem so much older.

We finished eating and Caeden took our plates to rinse off and put in the dishwasher. Moments like this made it so easy to forget all the bad going on in our lives. In these brief times, we were just Caeden and Sophie—husband and wife—going about our daily activities and being *normal*. I craved normalcy something fierce. But the moment I found out I was a shifter, any chance at a normal life went out the window, and honestly when it came down to it, I wouldn't have it any other way. Caeden, the whole pack, the shifting, all of it was amazing and it was worth the bad times. After all, once Travis was gone once and for all our lives could be—not normal—but peaceful.

"What are you smiling about?" Caeden asked.

"I didn't realize I was."

"Well, you are," he chuckled, still waiting for an answer.

I thought for a moment before answering. "I guess...I'm just happy. Despite everything we've been through and everything we have yet to face, I am happy, and that's what matters."

He braced his hands on the counter and tilted his head, a slow smile lighting his face. "You're happy...it's good to hear that..." He paused, as if unsure if he should continue. "I've never doubted you loved me, Soph, but I have questioned your happiness. You've been through a lot, and all of it has been because of me. So many things could have been avoided if we weren't mates."

"Don't think for one *second* that I regret my fate." I stood and made my way to him. He opened his arms and I wrapped mine around him. I inhaled his woodsy scent, letting his warmth wash over me. "You and me, we're meant to be, and those hardships we've faced, they're merely bumps in the road. Together, we're unstoppable."

His lips brushed over my hair. "Unstoppable," he whispered.

We stood like that for several more minutes until he finally let me go.

"Well," he put his hands on his hips, "I guess I better see if I can find pumpkins since *someone* waited till the last minute to have the brilliant idea of carving them."

I laughed, my eyes darting down to the floor as I lifted my shoulders in a small shrug. "It didn't occur to me before."

"I'll be back soon," he stepped forward and took my chin between his fingers, placing a chaste kiss on my lips.

As he started out of the kitchen, I called after him, "Don't forget to get one for Nolan."

He chuckled in reply. "You got it."

Since I didn't feel like going back upstairs and lying in bed for hours, I decided to spend some time in the family room. I'd still be off my feet and bored out of my mind, but at least I'd have something different to look at.

I had just sat down and draped a blanket around my shoulders when Archie and Murphy joined me. Each dog took a spot beside me. They rarely left my side these days, even Murphy. I scratched the top of Archie's head and he leaned into my touch. I did the same for Archie before putting a movie on. There was never anything good to watch on TV. It was all either reruns or crazy people fighting over some random piece of crap. If I had to watch ladies fight over a something ridiculous one more time…

"Watcha doin'?" I looked up to see Nolan standing in the doorway. I swear he appeared out of nowhere all the time. It was like his super power or something.

"Watching a movie." I gave him a "duh" look. I mean, really, wasn't it obvious what I was doing? Why did I need to spell it out?

"Mind if I join you?"

"Uh…"

He must have taken that as a yes, because he said, "I'm going to pop some popcorn and be right back. Don't start it yet."

"You don't even know what I'm watching," I mumbled under my breath. I was suddenly mad that I'd picked Lord of the Rings to watch and not some flowery girl movie that would've been sure to scare Nolan away. But it was too late now to change it, because he'd hear me get up and know what I was doing. And while I was wary of Nolan, he wasn't a bad guy…at least as far as I knew.

He came in with a big bowl of popcorn and sat down so Archie was between us. "You can start it now," he mumbled as he shoved a handful of butter drenched popcorn in his mouth. "Want some?" He held the giant bowl out to me. He must have popped three bags of popcorn because I knew there was no way one bag produced that much.

"Uh, sure," I reached out and grabbed a handful.

It felt weird to be sitting here eating popcorn and watching Lord of the Rings with Nolan of all people. I didn't know him…and I guess that was my fault. I talked to him, sure, but not very much. And I'd been fine with him before Caeden said he thought there was a mole. But now, I wasn't sure if he was trustworthy. I was being unfair to him. I knew that. If there was a mole, which we didn't really know, it could be anyone. Besides, Caeden seemed convinced that the mole was a member of the elders.

I decided to relax and enjoy the movie despite Nolan's presence. Until the guy gave me a reason not to trust him, I should be more accommodating, and he'd always been nice to me.

We were halfway through the second movie when Caeden finally arrived home.

"Cay-berry! Does it really take that long to get pumpkins?" Nolan called out, throwing his arms in the air enthusiastically. I was about to ask Nolan how he knew about the pumpkins when I realized he's a shifter so of course he heard. With the loss of my abilities, I had forgotten that everyone else still had theirs.

"It does when every place I stopped had already packed up their pumpkins, since it's Halloween and all." Caeden appeared in the doorway.

"Did you not get any?" I frowned, noting his empty hands.

"Oh, I did. I got big ones...and I did manage to find a small one for the baby. They're in the kitchen."

I clapped my hands together. "Let's gut some pumpkins."

"Dude, you married a weird one," Nolan chuckled as he shook his head, his sandy hair falling in his eyes.

"I know, but I love her," Caeden winked at me.

"Weird one is sitting right here," I pointed at myself.

Caeden chuckled and his gaze flicked to the paused TV screen. "You guys are watching Lord of the Rings?"

"Yeah," I shrugged. "I was in the mood for something different."

Caeden shook his head. "Are we going to carve pumpkins or not?"

I hopped up—well, I got up as fast as I could which really wasn't all that fast. "A pumpkin carving we go," I saluted my husband as I passed him.

Since I was so weak, Caeden had to help me 'gut' my pumpkin, but once the top was off and the gunk was cleared out I started carving my design. I was no artist so I stuck with the simple design of a basic flower. I was happy with it until I saw Nolan's.

"Whoa," I gasped.

"You like it?" He asked with a grin.

I nodded. He'd carved the face of a tiger into the pumpkin and no detail had gone unnoticed. It was amazing and I couldn't wait to see it lit up. "It's incredible," I told him.

"Geez," Caeden glanced over, taking in Nolan's design, "and here I thought my wolf was going to impress you."

I snorted at Caeden's pathetic attempt to carve a wolf. It looked more like a mammoth or something. There was nothing about it that was remotely wolf like.

"That's…interesting," I said so as not to hurt his feelings.

He dropped the knife and it clanged on the countertop. "That's code for 'it sucks,'" he shook his head.

"It doesn't suck it just—"

"Sucks," Nolan finished for me and I sent him a glare.

"No, it doesn't," I continued to glare at him. "It's whimsical."

"You don't need to make me feel better, Soph. I'm a big boy. I can handle the truth," Caeden sighed, frowning at his pumpkin. "I never was much good at carving pumpkins. I once threw one at Bryce's head."

I giggled. "And what happened?"

"It bounced off because his head is full of air," he laughed, "and then my mom grounded me for two months."

Nolan and I burst into laughter.

"I remember that!" Nolan chortled. "I came over the next day and your mom was so pissed she wouldn't even let me in the house to give you your games back. She told me to keep them, because you were never allowed to do anything fun ever again."

"She was mad for a few days," Caeden continued to chuckle. "I don't know why though. It didn't hurt him. I'm not sure anything can hurt Bryce. He's indestructible or something."

"Maybe all those bad jokes he tells acts as a shield," I wiped tears from my eyes. I hadn't laughed like this in a very long time and it felt so, so good.

"They probably do," Caeden agreed, "they're pretty awful. Do you know what Lucinda told me?"

I shook my head.

"She caught Bryce taking a cupcake order and when he answered the phone, he said, "This is Bryce, thanks for calling Beaumont Sperm bank, you jack it we pack it.""

"He. Didn't." I gasped.

"Oh, he did. She fired him for it."

"When did this happen?" I questioned. I felt so out of the loop on everything.

Caeden's brow furrowed as he thought. "About a week ago."

I sighed. "I miss everything," I grumbled.

"Aw, Soph," Caeden reached over and rubbed my back, "that's not true."

"But it is," I groaned. "You're free to do whatever you want, go wherever you want, and see whoever you want. While I'm stuck here being an incubator." I realized the harshness of my words and glanced down at my tiny bump. "Sorry, baby, mommy didn't mean that."

"I know it sucks for you," Caeden reached for my hand, "but it's what's best for you and the baby right now."

"I know," I sighed. "But when we find out if it's a boy or a girl you can't stop me from shopping for baby clothes. It's happening."

He chuckled. "I'm sure we can arrange that."

Nolan fake gagged. Caeden and I turned to look at him. "When the mushiness starts that's my cue to leave."

"What was mushy about that?" Caeden asked.

"You're talking about a baby, before I know it you'll both be talking in high pitched baby voices. Give me one of those so I can light this damn jack o' lantern," Nolan pointed at the bag of tea lights.

Caeden tossed him the bag and he grabbed the pumpkin, heading for the front door.

"I guess we better finish this one," I pointed at the small pumpkin meant for the baby.

"You better do it," he spun his pumpkin around. "I'll just butcher it."

"Whatever, Negative Nancy." I reached for the knife and set about carving an antique baby rattle. It seemed simple enough, but it ended up looking like a weird balloon with a handle. "Eh, good enough," I shrugged. "We can't all be artists like Nolan. After all, it's the effort and thought that counts."

Caeden grabbed our pumpkins and I carried the baby one out to the front porch. Nolan was still outside, admiring his pumpkin. Weirdo.

Caeden lit the little candles in the jack o' lanterns and we stood back to admire our handy work—or in this case *not* so handy work.

Nolan snorted at our pathetic attempt at a jack o' lantern. "Be thankful you don't have to be an artist to be Alpha," Nolan clapped Caeden on the shoulder as he shook his head.

Caeden shrugged off Nolan's hand. "Luckily I'm very skilled at more useful things."

Nolan chuckled, glancing from Caeden to me. "Oh, I'm sure you are, Cay-berry. I'm sure you are."

With that he sauntered forward and into the house.

Caeden shook his head at Nolan's words. With a sigh he reached for my hand and pulled me against his side. I let his warmth envelope me and tried to enjoy this moment of peace, they were few and far between.

I knew Sophie needed to feel normal, even if that meant carving the ugliest pumpkins on the planet. I knew the pregnancy was hard on her and she hated feeling useless, but I'd never forgive myself if I let her over exert herself and it ended up hurting her or the baby.

I let her enjoy the fresh air for a few minutes before coaxing her inside.

I honestly couldn't believe that it was already Halloween. Time was passing by way faster than I wanted it to. I felt so unprepared—not only with Travis and his mutants but with the baby as well. My dad had been a great role model, but that didn't prepare me for the profoundness of having a kid. I was going to have a little human-being dependent on me to keep her alive. How crazy was that? Especially when I couldn't seem to keep my pack alive. I rubbed my jaw, and turned to Sophie, hoping I could get my mind on other things.

"How about we finish that movie?"

"But...you weren't watching it. You'll be confused," her nose crinkled with the cold air.

I laughed heartily at that. "Babe, I've seen that movie so many times I have it memorized."

That got her to smile. God, I loved that smile, and these days seeing it was a rarity.

"I'd like that." She wrapped her arms around her torso as she shivered from the cool night air.

I held the door open for her and followed her into the family room.

My eyes scanned her body—but not for the reason you'd think. She looked...thinner. But how was that possible? Weren't you supposed to gain weight when you're pregnant?

I shook my head, sure I was just imagining things. Surely she wasn't losing weight. I mean, she had a baby bump and she was eating regularly. Now, I was just inventing stuff to worry about.

Sophie grabbed a blanket and wrapped it around herself before plopping dramatically onto the couch. "You coming?" She asked when she looked up and saw me standing in the archway.

I nodded and strode forward. I sat down beside her and pulled her into my arms. She came eagerly. I loved being close to her like this. I really missed these moments. We rarely had them anymore. Everything was always so serious now.

"You starting the movie back up?" Nolan asked a moment before he appeared.

I nodded.

"Sweet," he jumped onto the couch and bounced a few times. He grabbed a pillow and adjusted it behind his head.

I knew there were a million other things I should have been doing, especially since I'd lost so much time hunting down and carving pumpkins, but right now I needed this. I kissed the top of Sophie's head and wiggled around until I found a comfortable spot. I needed times like these to remind me what I was fighting so hard for.

* * *

The movie ended and Sophie had fallen asleep. Her head was propped on my arm and drool had leaked from the corner of her mouth onto my shirt. At least she was cute, so I couldn't be pissed.

I stood, careful to keep a hand on her so she didn't fall over. I carefully wrapped my arms around her and pulled her against my chest. "Night," I nodded at Nolan as I headed out of the room carrying my sleeping wife. I laid her down in bed and removed her jeans. I knew from experience that sleeping in jeans wasn't fun. I brought the blankets up around her and gazed down at her sleeping form.

A dark brown lock of hair fell over her forehead and her pale pink lips were slightly pouted in sleep. She was the most beautiful woman I had ever laid eyes on, and she was mine. That fact would never cease to amaze me.

I bent down and lightly brushed my lips against hers. She stirred in her sleep, making a content humming noise in her throat. Her lashes fluttered against her cheeks and she settled once more.

I slowly backed out of the room, careful to keep my movements silent.

I eased the door closed and let out the breath I'd been holding.

I headed to my office and collapsed in the chair behind my desk. This house, this life, it didn't seem like mine. I'd accepted my dad's death and the responsibility that came with it. But there was so much more to being Alpha that you couldn't comprehend until you were living it.

I swallowed thickly, replaying the events of summer and the wolves we lost. I cared for them all, but losing Logan had hit me the hardest, obviously. We'd grown up together and I'd never thought I could lose him or any of them. That had been immature of me. We were shifters but we weren't invincible. Our hearts beat and blood ran through our veins. We were *alive* and life can be snuffed out in an instant. I knew Soph still beat herself up over Logan's death and I did too. I didn't think there would ever be a day that I *didn't* think of Logan. At least I hoped not. I never wanted to forget him—any of them—and the sacrifice he made. I missed him, but he saved my she-wolf, and I'd be lost without her. I owed him everything. I hoped that wherever he was, he knew how grateful I was.

The door to my office creaked open and my head snapped up. I didn't like being caught off guard. I looked up, expecting to see Sophie, but instead my eyes met Nolan's.

"What are you doing?" He asked. "Meditating or something? That's really a pussy thing to do."

I leaned back in my chair and glared at him. Sometimes Nolan got on my nerves as much as Bryce did. "No," I drew out the word, "I was thinking."

"About what?" He prodded with his beefy arms crossed over his chest. For anyone that didn't know Nolan, he looked like an intimidating guy, but he wasn't.

"Don't you have someone else to bug?" I snapped.

I was sick and tired of everyone asking me so many questions. I wanted to be left alone and that didn't seem like a lot to ask for.

"No, you're my victim of choice tonight," Nolan swaggered further into my office with a gleam in his eyes. Great, I'd just given him a challenge.

"Yeah, well, without me you don't have a roof over your head," I lifted my arms in the air.

Nolan narrowed his eyes. "Cay-berry, you're smart enough to know that threats don't work with me."

"It was worth a shot," I shrugged, my sigh echoing around the room.

"So," Nolan plopped in the chair in front of my desk and rubbed his hands on his jeans, "talk Cay-berry."

I growled at the ridiculous name.

"I have all night," Nolan looked around, "and tomorrow, and the next day, and the next—"

"I get it," I held up a hand to shut him up. Honestly, the dude needed to come with an off switch or a button that switched him from annoying to tolerable. "I was just thinking about Logan."

"Logan? Why?" Nolan's brows furrowed together until they looked like a hairy caterpillar sitting on his face.

"I don't know," I said sarcastically, "maybe because he's dead."

"Dude, that was a while ago," Nolan relaxed in the chair.

"A while ago?" I couldn't believe him. "It was only this past summer!"

He gave a small shrug and the movement only made me want to reach across and punch him in the face. "Caeden," I was shocked he used my real name, "we're shifters. Tragic deaths is part of the card we're dealt," he rubbed his jaw. "You've read the legends, you know that packs used to fight to the death over minor disagreements. All shifters are volatile by nature. You might think you're a nice guy, Cay-berry, but under that sweet exterior," he looked me up and down, "you're a beast. We all are. Some of us are just worse than others, like Travis."

I ground my teeth together. I didn't like it when Nolan made sense.

"I'm nothing like Travis."

"You've killed, haven't you?" Nolan countered.

I felt sweat bead on my forehead. "In self defense! I haven't gone out and killed innocent people like he has! There's a big difference!"

"Is there?" He threaded his fingers together and suddenly I felt like I was being analyzed by a psychologist or something. "A life is a life, no matter whose life it is."

A life is a life, no matter whose life it is. I replayed his words over again in my head. He was right. I was a killer, like Travis. Travis had gotten what he wanted. He'd made me into him. I was tainted now.

And I knew I'd kill him and whoever stood in my way to keep my family and pack safe.

If that made me a bad person, I didn't care.

"I did what I had to do," I finally said.

Nolan shrugged. "So was the mutant that killed Logan. We all have a role to play in this world. Some of us get to be the good guys, but most of us our bad guys. You and me," Nolan stood and looked down at me, "we're bad guys, Caeden. But not for the reason you think."

"Explain then," I growled.

"We're bad," he said slowly so I heard every word clearly, "because we'll protect what belongs to us, no matter the cost. We don't care who gets hurt and who stands in our way. We're loyal to a fault, Caeden. Why do you think I'm here?"

"I-I-don't know," I shook my head. "To help us?" It came out as a question.

"That's part of it," he shrugged, "but it all boys down to loyalty, Caeden. I know if I needed your help you'd be there in a heartbeat and I'd do the same for you."

"Yeah, but you've been gone for years, Nolan!" I cried.

He looked at me sadly. "I know. And I'm sorry for that."

"Are you ever going to tell me what happened?"

I was desperate to know what had sent Nolan running from our lives. Nolan was a tough guy so it had to be something bad. I could speculate about his reasons all I wanted, but until he told me I'd never know for sure.

"Let's put it this way," he started towards the door, "I was given a choice and I made the wrong one. Running was the only way to survive."

NINE.
Sophie

"Everything looks excellent," Dr. James rolled the wand over my stomach. "The baby's growing at the perfect pace and its heart sounds strong. I'm very pleased with how things are coming along. But how are *you* feeling?" He asked, removing the wand and returning it to the station.

"Tired," I shrugged. I couldn't go into details with him of everything I was experiencing.

He tilted his head and studied me for a moment. "You're young, so your body should be better equipped to handle a pregnancy. Tiredness is normal but if this is an ongoing problem…" He trailed off, waiting for me to reply.

"No, no, it just happens occasionally," I lied, using the paper sheet to wipe the goo off my belly.

"Sophie, I'm your doctor, I need you to be completely honest with me. If you're not, I can't help you."

"I am being honest. I told you I was tired…occasionally."

He sighed and I knew he wasn't buying what I was saying. "You need to get plenty of rest, and if you continue to feel tired I want you to make an emergency appointment, because it might mean something is wrong."

I nodded as he continued to stare at me. Satisfied with what he saw, he turned and grabbed the newest sonogram. "Here's your baby."

I stared down at the grainy image. The baby no longer looked like a misshapen gray blob. It was obviously a baby. My baby. I ran my finger over the cute bump of its nose and the curve of its pouty lips. It was the most perfect baby I'd ever seen and I hadn't even technically laid eyes on it.

"Thank you, Dr. James," Caeden stood and shook his hand.

The doctor left the room and I hopped down to put my pants back on.

"Can we *please* go somewhere for a little bit?" I begged. "We don't have to be gone long. I'm just not ready to go home yet."

Caeden sighed and pinched the bridge of his nose. I knew he was caving to my pleas. I was going stir crazy and if I didn't get to do something fun soon, I might kill someone.

"Why don't we go to Target and look at baby things?" He suggested. "You get out and we're doing something productive."

"Sounds perfect," I grinned, resisting the urge to jump up and down.

"But we can only look for thirty minutes, any longer than that is too long for you to be on your feet," he warned.

"Thirty minutes is fine with me," I pulled my jacket on.

Caeden shook his head and grumbled under his breath. "What have I gotten myself into?"

"Oh, come on, it won't be that bad," I patted his scruffy cheek in a loving manner. "Don't you want to help me pick out baby stuff?"

"Of course," he shrugged. "I just don't want you to wear yourself out."

I didn't either. But I needed to get out and breathe in fresh air and see something other than the inside of my house.

"I'll be fine," I kissed him before opening the door.

We walked out of the doctor's office and Caeden held open the Jeep's passenger door for me. He held out his hand as I climbed into the high vehicle. I had never had trouble getting in and out of his Jeep before, but right now it was a struggle.

"To Target we go," Caeden sighed as he pulled out of the parking lot.

It took us a good twenty minutes to get to the store and I rode with the window cracked slightly so that the cool air could blow in and tickle my face. There were so many things I had taken for granted before I was trapped in my own house. I knew I was doing what was best for the baby and me by limiting my activity, but that didn't make it any easier. Everyone wants to get out now and then.

"You okay?" Caeden asked as I rolled the window up before he turned off the car.

"Yeah," I replied, wondering how many more times he was going to ask me that before we made it home.

"I'm not sure this is a good idea," he looked at the store and back at me, nervously chewing on his bottom lip.

I chose to ignore him and got out of the car.

"Soph," he grumbled as we walked towards the entrance, "you should have waited for me to help you."

"It sounded to me like you were talking yourself out of letting me go in. I wasn't going to risk you racing out of the parking lot like a crazy person," I glared at him as I wrapped my arms around my body. I was so cold. I hated it.

Inside the store, Caeden grabbed one of the red shopping carts and headed straight for the baby department. It wasn't hard to find since it was right in front of the store.

I picked up a little onesie with yellow ducks and marveled at the small size of it. Would our baby really be that tiny? What if I broke it? I mean, something that small had to be incredibly delicate.

I suddenly wished I was like other girls and had experience with babysitting. At least then I'd know what I was doing. Instead, I was going to have a baby and be absolutely clueless. You know, nothing they taught you in school ever turned out to be useful in real life. I really hoped 'motherly instinct' was a real thing and I'd be fine, because all this tiny stuff everywhere was really scaring the crap out of me.

"Hey, Sophie! Look at this!" Caeden held up a small hat that was made to look like a wolf. "The baby has to have this."

"I thought the baby was a girl," I taunted him. "That looks like something a boy would wear."

He frowned down at the hat. "I don't care. I'm buying it."

I ran my fingers over more of the clothes as I passed by. I saw strollers and carseats ahead of me and that didn't seem as scary as the clothes.

I began reading the descriptions of the various carriers and decided that these were as scary as the clothes, if not more. How on earth did you decide which one was the safest for your child?

I was beginning to regret agreeing to come here. All of this stuff was frightening me. I looked down the aisle at Caeden who was checking out a stroller. He seemed completely at ease. How unfair was that? Wasn't it the man that was supposed to freak out over baby stuff, not the woman? Leave it to me to go against the grain.

"Soph, I think this is a good one," Caeden called, removing his black baseball cap and ruffling his hair before replacing it backwards.

I made my way towards him and shrugged at the stroller. "Why?"

"Well, it's sturdy for one," he pointed, "it comes with a carrier and you can convert it when the baby gets too big for a carrier. It's also unisex, just in case Lucy turns out to be Beau."

My eyes watered. That was the first time, since the day we discussed names, that either of us had mentioned them. I felt a rush of emotion pour over me that was unlike anything I'd ever felt. Baby, wasn't just *baby*, it was either *Lucy* or *Beau*.

"Soph…" Caeden said my name slowly. "You okay?"

I nodded, wiping away the one tear that had managed to escape. "Yeah, sorry."

"Are you sure you're okay? Why are you crying?"

"Just overly emotional," I shrugged, taking a deep breath to calm myself.

He frowned and a wrinkle marred his forehead. Finally, he said, "If it's about the stroller, we don't have to get this one. You can pick the one you want."

"This one is perfect," I told him.

He grinned and pulled the large box off the shelf. It dropped into the cart with a bang.

"Caeden!" I scolded.

He chuckled. "Sorry."

Since my thirty minutes were almost up I scanned all the aisles. I picked up a set of assorted onesies that would work for a boy or girl, a pale green blanket, and a pack of little socks. I knew it wasn't much, but it felt good to buy stuff for the baby. I couldn't wait to find out the gender so I could buy more clothes and decorate the nursery. I admired the couples who could wait to find out the gender. I *had* to know. It was killing me to wait and we still had a good month to go.

Which reminded me…

"What are we doing for Thanksgiving?" I questioned Caeden as we headed for a checkout line. Unfortunately everyone seemed to be checking out at the same time. This was going to take forever. "Are we going to your mom's?"

He shrugged and scratched his stubbled chin. "I haven't thought about it. I assume we're going to my mom's but…oh, crap."

"What?"

"It's pack tradition to gather at the Alpha's house for Thanksgiving," he swallowed thickly.

This was definitely crap-worthy news.

"Caeden, I can't stand and cook all day."

"I know that," he sighed. "I'm sure mom won't mind cooking it, but it'll look bad if we don't have it at our house."

"*Great,*" I rolled my eyes. This was exactly what I didn't need. Having the whole pack over would mean a full house and me having to act like everything was fine. Caeden didn't want anyone knowing about how difficult my pregnancy was. Only Gram, Nolan, Caeden's mom, and Chris knew about it...and even Chris hadn't been told the whole truth. I hated keeping things from my friends and family. It didn't make me feel good.

"It'll be okay," Caeden cupped my cheek.

"That's easy for you to say," I countered. "You don't have anything to hide." I frowned, looking around so I didn't have to meet his gaze.

"I have everything to hide," he growled quietly. "I have to go on and act like I have everything under control— like I don't believe there's a target on my back," his voice was fierce.

I took a deep breath and pushed my hair out of my eyes. "You're right. We're both stuck in this predicament together. I *hate* this."

"I know you do, and I don't like it either. But for now, I don't have proof that the elders want me dead and I don't know what Travis is up to. But I still have to act level-headed and not like I'm afraid of my own shadow," he hissed through gritted teeth.

"Are you?"

"Am I what?" His brows furrowed together.

"Afraid of your own shadow?"

"Right now, I am," he answered honestly. "I don't know who trust."

And that right there was what everything boiled down to. Anyone could be an enemy, and that was a really scary thought.

TEN.
Sophie

I stared out the bedroom window. Crinkly brown leaves blew in the wind, swirling around before settling until another breeze came along. I wished I could blow away and pretend this whole nightmare was over.

Pack members were arriving for Thanksgiving dinner and I wanted nothing more to hide here for the rest of the evening. Normally, I couldn't wait to leave this bedroom. It had become my prison. But right now, I'd gladly be trapped here then have to smile and act like everything was okay when it definitely wasn't. I was no actress and I wasn't sure I could do it. I'd helped Amy cook several of the dishes but I excused myself over an hour ago with the excuse that I'd needed to get ready. Had I done that? No. Instead I'd laid down, paced the room, and stared out the window for the last sixty minutes. I was a productive person like that...not. I was surprised Caeden hadn't come up here and hunted me down yet. I guess he was too busy greeting everyone. I knew the responsible thing to do was be by his side, but I just couldn't do it. I wasn't cut out for this life. I didn't grow up knowing I was a shifter and I hadn't been prepared to lead a pack. Caeden had grown up fully aware of his responsibilities and even he had trouble accepting it. But he was better at this than I was. If I was down there right now I'd just be standing beside him uncomfortably, most likely not saying a word. I didn't really know our pack that well. I was only close with our generation pack. I'd been introduced to our friends parents, and met them a few times, but I still didn't feel comfortable around them...especially since it felt like one of them should be Alpha not Caeden and I. I had accepted our responsibility and I *was* an Alpha. Power ran through my veins and it wasn't a position I could just give up. But sometimes it felt like we weren't ready for this. We'd already made so many mistakes and lives had been lost because of it.

I placed my hand against the glass, fighting tears.

Logan.

He wouldn't be here with us today. I'd have to look at Chris and her *parents* and know that because of me they no longer had their brother and son. They probably wished on a daily basis that I was dead. I didn't blame them.

"Sophie?"

I cringed. I wasn't ready to be found yet.

"Yes?" I didn't bother to turn away from the window at the sound of Caeden's voice.

"Almost everyone is here. You need to come downstairs."

I shook my head. "I can't."

"You *have* to," he growled.

"Caeden," I turned away from the window and he saw the tears staining my cheeks, "I'm telling you I can't do this. For once, just leave me alone!"

He walked forward and enveloped me in his arms. I didn't want to respond to his touch, but my body had a mind of its own.

"Let me go," I said weakly.

"You know you don't want that," he chuckled, his lips brushing against the top of my head. My eyes fluttered closed and my body began to relax. I didn't want him to calm me though. I wanted to stay up here and wallow.

After a few minutes he pulled away. He cupped my face between his large hands and gazed down at me. "Come on, where's my she-wolf?"

"Your she-wolf is gone," I sighed. "She can't even shift anymore."

"You're too hard on yourself, Soph." He smiled at me and said, "Change into something nice and come downstairs for dinner."

"I can't face all of them. I *can't* see Logan's parents. I just can't do it, Caeden. I can't." I kept repeating the words over and over again, hoping they'd get through to him and he'd understand.

"Oh, Sophie," he breathed, "you have got to let this go and move beyond it. We're shifters, we all know from a young age that we might die in a fight of some sort. Logan made his choice. *His choice*, Sophie. Not my choice. Not your choice. But *his* choice. He died for you and instead of sulking like you stuck a blade in his heart, you need to put a smile on your face and show his parent's that his death wasn't in vain."

"I hate it when you're right," I forced a small smile.

"*When* I'm right? Baby, I'm always right."

"I'll be downstairs in a few minutes," I backed away from him and towards the closet.

"I'll wait for you," he sat on the bed, watching me carefully like he thought I was going to make a run for it and jump out the window.

"You don't need to do that. I'm just going to change," I shrugged, stepping into the large walk-in closest.

"Yes, I do."

His tone of voice was stern so I knew there was no point in arguing. "Okay."

I found a clingy black dress that hugged my expanding curves, but didn't make me feel like I was being suffocated. I paired it with simple black flats and left my hair down to swish around my shoulders.

"That didn't take long," Caeden commented when I stepped back into the bedroom.

"That's all I get?"

"You look beautiful," he grinned crookedly, his dimple winking at me. I liked it when he smiled like that. A *real* smile. He didn't do it enough anymore.

"That's better," I laughed.

We made our way downstairs and I prepared myself to face everyone. My breathing was labored and I was tempted to turn around and run away. But that was weak, and I wasn't a victim. I think my pregnancy hormones were messing with me. I'd went from being someone who was a fighter to a sniveling baby over night. I needed to get my spark back.

"Ready?" Caeden asked before we rounded the corner that opened into the dining room.

"Yes," I answered, even though I was far from ready.

Apparently, while Caeden was gone retrieving me, everyone had arrived. The room was packed and I wondered if we had enough room for everyone. Gosh, there were a lot of them.

"Hi," I waved my hand awkwardly.

Several of the members I'd never been formally introduced to gazed at me curiously while others tossed glares my way. I felt like a tiny insect being scrutinized beneath the lens of a microscope. I didn't like it one bit. I'd never been one to enjoy being the center of attention and to have this many eyes on me was a bit unnerving.

I swallowed the lump in my throat as my heart beat abnormally fast in my chest like a fluttery bird trying to escape the confines of its cage.

Caeden cleared his throat. "Sophie and I are happy that so many of you were able to join us this Thanksgiving— our first as husband and wife," he gave my shoulder a squeeze. "We've all been through a lot since last years dinner. Some, unfortunately, aren't here to enjoy this meal and their presence will be missed. The threat is still out there, but I know together we can eliminate it. To strength," Caeden reached over and grabbed a glass off the table, which he lifted in the air.

Everyone did the same, echoing his words.

After that, Caeden pulled out a chair for me beside his place at the head of the table.

The food was passed around and I piled a spoonful of everything onto my plate. Amy was an incredible cook and I devoured my plate in no time. It was unladylike of me, but whatever. I was hungry…and pregnant, so I had an excuse.

Luckily our friends were seated beside us so I didn't have to make small talk with a stranger.

"How's married life treating you?" I asked Bentley and Christian who sat across from me.

Bentley's entire face lit up and his brown eyes sparkled with excitement. I'd never seen him look so excited before. "It's wonderful. Who wouldn't love waking up to this face every morning?" He poked Chris' cheek.

She rolled her eyes and swatted his hand away. "He just likes the constant sex."

I choked on the piece of broccoli I was eating. Leave it to Christian to take this conversation into awkward territory. I was ready to back peddle out of this.

"I don't have to married to have constant sex," Bryce piped in.

I looked beside me to see Charlotte's whole face flushed red. "Shut up," she hissed under her breath at Bryce.

Bryce smirked and draped his arm over the top of her chair.

"We ain't got nothin' to be ashamed of," he put his other hand on his chest, "sex is a natural part of life." Dang, he sounded like a strung out hippie. "Thunder has to have some lovin'," he chuckled.

"Oh my God, kill me now," Charlotte hung her head in her hands. "I'm not very hungry anymore," she dropped her napkin on her plate and pushed it away.

"Hungry for something else?" Bryce waggled his brows.

"I'm going to kill you in your sleep," she warned, narrowing her eyes at him. "I will literally sneak into your room and slit your throat."

"Baby, if you wanted it rough all you had to do is ask, no need to be so angry about it. Although, I'm not down for throat slitting. That usually ends in death and death is *so* not cool."

"I don't know why I love you," she shook her head.

I honestly didn't know how Charlotte tolerated Bryce. Don't get me wrong, I loved Bryce to death, but he had no filter and Charlotte was the more shy type. They were complete opposites, but they always say opposites attract. I guess only time would tell where those two ended up.

Bryce opened up his mouth, no doubt to say something else equally disgusting, but Caeden glared at his younger brother. "Say one more word and I'll put you in the corner like the five year old you act like."

"Dude, chill," Bryce raised his hands in the air in mock surrender. "You're not my dad, you don't need to use that tone with me."

"Someone has to," Caeden grumbled. "You're embarrassing me and you're embarrassing your girlfriend."

By this time the table was quieting and people were starting to look toward our end of the table.

Bryce knew better than to say anything further, so his only form of defiance was saluting Caeden, like he was a drill sergeant.

Caeden shook his head and let out a deep breath. I knew he wanted to avoid a scene in front of a crowd like this. Leave it to Bryce to stir up trouble. I know Bryce always meant everything in jest, but sometimes he really needed to think things through before he said them. He was the Alpha's brother and so he was under just as much scrutiny by the elders as we were.

Luckily we made it through dinner and desert without any more outbursts from Bryce or anyone else. People slowly began to leave and Amy stayed behind to help us clean things up. My parents and Gram left earlier. I had hugged them tightly, never wanting to let go. I hadn't seen Gram since the day she told us about the baby draining me and I hadn't seen my parents since my first ultrasound appointment. I missed them fiercely, but since I couldn't talk to them about what was going on, I decided distance was better. Maybe that made me a wimp, but I didn't care. It seemed wrong keeping things from them and I knew if I was around them too much I'd end up spilling the beans about the baby, and since Caeden didn't want anything getting back to the elders there wasn't much I could talk to Gram about. I mean, she did know about the baby, and obviously hadn't said anything, but Caeden was so freakin' paranoid. God, he needed a chill pill...or three.

I finished loading the last dish in the dishwasher and turned to Amy. "Thanks for staying to help clean up and cooking the meal. It was delicious. It meant a lot to me."

"It was no trouble at all," she smiled kindly. "I was happy to help."

We stood, not saying anything for a moment. I'd always liked Amy. She was a good mom and she had always been kind to me. I was really lucky to have her in my life.

"Do you..." She trailed off. "Do you mind?"

My brows furrowed in confusion and then I looked at her hands, noting that she wanted to touch my expanding bump. "Of course," I replied with a smile.

Her hands tentatively cupped my small rounded stomach. A slow smile spread across her face. "I can't believe I'm going to be a grandma. I feel too young," she laughed, looking up at me with kind blue eyes.

"I know exactly what you mean. *I* feel too young for this. A baby is a huge responsibility, but I love her already."

She laughed. "Caeden told me he thinks it's a girl."

"Yeah, I'm not convinced, but I didn't like calling the baby 'it'. That seemed wrong," I shrugged as her hands dropped away from my belly.

"I feel like I never see you two anymore," Amy frowned. "You and Caeden should come over for dinner one evening."

"I'd like that. I'll talk to him about it," I assured her as I followed her out of the kitchen. With how exhausted I'd been, I doubted dinner would happen anytime soon. She grabbed her coat and shrugged into it before wrapping a fluffy red scarf around her neck. "Well, I better get going."

"Thank you, again," I reached out and hugged her.

"You're welcome," she hugged me back tightly.

I locked the door behind her and trudged up to bed. Today had really taken a toll on me. Not only was my body exhausted, but my brain was tired too from all the endless thoughts that had been running through my mind.

Caeden was taking a shower and since I knew I was too tired to rinse away the days grime, I just got in my pajamas, climbed into bed and promptly fell asleep.

* * *

Caeden

"Wake up, Sophie," I shook her sleeping form. "Wake up. Wake up. Wake up!" I pleaded. She'd been asleep for two whole days! I should have just said screw it and not hosted the Thanksgiving dinner, but as Alpha that was my responsibility. But now Sophie wouldn't wake up.

"Dude, stop shaking her like that. That can't be good for her," Nolan warned as he appeared in the doorway.

I laced my hands behind my head and paced the length of the bedroom. "She won't wake up."

"I kind of figured that out," Nolan gave me an arrogant smirk. I was so angry that I was tempted to punch him in the face.

"I don't have time for your sarcasm. I need to wake Sophie up."

89

"I think you need to chill," Nolan said. I turned around to continue my pacing, but his hand slammed roughly into my shoulder, halting my progress.

"Two days," I cried. "It's been two freakin' days and she's *still* sleeping!"

"Obviously this is what her body needs," Nolan's voice was annoyingly calm and devoid of emotion. "You could cause more harm than good by waking her up."

I squished my eyes closed and let out a growl. When Nolan started making sense you knew things were bad.

"I don't like this," I shook my head as my eyes popped open. "I don't like it one bit."

"You don't have to like it," Nolan said. "That's your wife and baby, you just accept it."

I let out a deep breath. "When did you get so smart?"

"I've always been this smart. You choose to ignore me. No hard feelings, Cay-berry," he clapped his hand on my shoulder and guided me out of the bedroom.

"I need to—"

"Nope!"

I strained against the hold he had on me, trying to get back to Sophie.

"Cay-berry, I will full on tackle you to the ground, tie you up, and drag you out of that room if you go in there to sulk for one more minute," Nolan warned.

"Point taken," I finally managed to get him to release his hold. Sophie's cellphone began to ring, and before Nolan could stop me I ran back into the bedroom and grabbed the thin device off the table. "Hello?"

"Caeden? Why are you answering Sophie's phone?" Evan asked.

"Oh, uh, she's busy right now," I stammered.

"Put her on the phone," Evan sounded exasperated.

"Seriously, she can't come to the phone right now, she's in the shower." I pinched the bridge of my nose. "What do you need?"

Evan sighed. "The guys and I are home for Thanksgiving break and wanted to see Sophie. We talked about it weeks ago."

Shit.

"When do you go back home?"

"Tomorrow morning."

Crap. Crap. Crap.

"Yeah, um, I don't think this is going to work out. Sorry, Evan, honestly."

"We're already on our way," Evan said. "It's not like it takes her five hours to shower."

"But we had plans," I lied.

"And now you have new ones," Evan sounded smug. "See you soon."

The call disconnected and I put the phone down before I crushed it in my palm.

Nolan snickered in the doorway. "Shouldn't have answered it, Cay-berry."

"Yeah, yeah, yeah," I braced my hands on my hips. "Now help me figure this out."

"Me? You're the one that lied," Nolan chuckled. "You are *so* on your own for this."

"Nolan!" I was tempted to punch him in the face. "I don't know what to do!"

I think that was the first time I'd admitted that aloud to anyone but Sophie. I knew my words were only about dealing with Evan and the other guys, but they extended beyond that. I had no idea what I was doing when it came to everything.

Nolan crossed his arms over his chest and laughed heartily. "Oh, I love this. Caeden Williams doesn't know what to do."

"They're going to be here any minute!" I was getting frantic now, which wasn't like me at all. But I couldn't have them finding Sophie passed out cold like this. They'd assume the worst. "They can't see her like this!"

Nolan tapped his chin thoughtfully. "Tell them she got out of her shower and is taking a nap. She's tired," he shrugged.

"Do you think that'll work?" It seemed too simple.

"I don't know why not."

I took a deep breath and nodded. "I'll try that."

The buzzer sounded that indicated someone at the gate wanting inside.

I headed downstairs to check the video feed and when I was sure it was Evan and the rest of the guys, I pushed the button that allowed them access. I waited by the front door and greeted them warmly.

"It's nice to see all of you. It's been too long."

"Where's the she-wolf?" Brody asked, pushing his black hair out of his eyes.

"I'm sorry guys but I didn't catch her in time. She's not feeling well so she got in the bed after her shower and she's passed out asleep."

"Oh," Evan sighed. "Well…"

I felt bad that they'd all come this far to see Sophie only to be disappointed. "You guys can wait as long as you want. She's been taking really long naps so if you're ready to leave and she's still not up, feel free to just leave."

Evan looked around at the rest of the guys. "Sounds good to us, as long as we aren't imposing."

"Not at all," I closed the door behind them. "Can I get you anything to drink?"

They all barked out different things at the same time. "Uh…I'll be back with that in a minute. Make yourself comfortable," I pointed into the family room.

Nolan cornered me in the kitchen where I was placing all the drinks on a tray. "Dude, they were going to leave! Why'd you ask them to stay?"

"It was the nice thing to do," I shrugged. "My mom and dad didn't raise me to be rude to people," I grumbled under my breath.

"It's not being rude, it's called being logical," Nolan groaned at my stupidity. "You know," he continued, "that's your problem. You need to toughen up."

"Huh?"

Nolan's fist cocked back and straight into my face. He packed enough force and I was caught off guard, so I fell to the ground.

"Did you really just punch me in the face?!" I yelled.

"I did. Punch me back, Cay-berry," he raised both his fists and danced on the balls of his feet.

"No way." I wasn't giving Nolan the reaction that he wanted from me. I was smarter than that.

"Come on, Cay-berry. *Fight back*. Prove to me that you're not the pansy you act like."

My nostrils flared at that.

"Prove that you're a man, Caeden. *Fight me*."

When I still didn't do anything, he drew his foot back and kicked my side. I had anticipated that, so the blow wasn't as hard as it could have been. He was really beginning to make me mad now, which was what he wanted.

"Get up, and fight me," he tilted his head, grinning manically.

I hopped to my feet in one lithe move and punched him in the nose. Blood trickled down to his chin. "That's more like it," he laughed. "There's the fire I want to see."

"You happy now?"

"Very," he grabbed a dishtowel off the counter and used it to clean his bloody nose.

I shook my head. "I don't understand what that was about."

"I wanted to see if you still had it," he shrugged.

"Have what?" Why the hell did Nolan always have to speak in damn riddles? Wasn't it easier to just say whatever you have to say?

"The *fire*," he spoke fiercely. "The drive to fight and conquer. You haven't been acting like a leader these last few months, Caeden. You've only thought about Sophie and holed up in your office doing God knows what. I wanted to see that your leader instincts were still there, and they are. So, congratulations, Caeden," he slow clapped.

"You make absolutely no sense whatsoever," I shook my head.

"I do make sense," he countered, "you're just too dense to see what I'm showing you."

"And what's that?"

"Do I really have to spell it out for you? Get with the program, Cay-berry," he smacked his hands in front of my face like you might do to someone who was staring off into space—only I wasn't.

Nothing else could be said because Evan chose that moment to step into the kitchen. "Everything alright?" He asked. "It was taking you a while to get the drinks and I heard raised voices..." He trailed off.

"Yeah, sorry," I shook my head, "the drinks are ready."

"Cool," Evan grabbed several of the drinks off the tray and I picked up the remaining few.

I decided to hang out with the guys, even though I felt incredibly awkward. They weren't my friends, they were Sophie's, but it would have been rude to ditch them. Nolan didn't join me. Figures.

I couldn't for the life of me figure out what he meant by punching me and by a *fire*, and so on. Nolan needed to come with an instruction book to decipher his alien messages.

"You said Sophie's napping?" Riley questioned.

I nodded.

"She sick?" He continued his inquisition as all of the guys stared me down. They acted like they thought I'd killed her and stuffed her body in a closet or something.

"Kind of," I shrugged, relaxing in the leather chair, the picture of ease. "She's having a hard time with the pregnancy."

Kyle, one of the guys that never seemed to say much, spat out sweet tea everywhere at my words. "Baby?"

"She's pregnant?" Evan choked, his eyes bugging out in shock.

"Uh...yeah...you didn't—uh—know?" I squirmed uncomfortably. Thank God Sophie had surprised me with the news of the baby in front of our whole family, because if telling her friends made me feel this uncomfortable, I hated to think of how I would've felt telling her dad.

"She never told us," Brody piped in. "She doesn't really talk to any of us that much anymore. I mean, we're off at college and she's here," he looked around at the large room. "I get it, I do. But we miss her." All the guys nodded in agreement.

His words made me feel bad, because they had been really good friends to Sophie. *Human* friends, and I knew she treasured them.

"There's been a lot going on," I explained. "The pregnancy has been...difficult." And wasn't that the understatement of the freakin' century.

"Is she okay? The baby?" Brody asked.

I nodded. "Yeah. Nothing *major* is wrong. She's just exhausted." And I was too. All the worrying I was doing was really taking a toll on me. I was going to have to get better about leaving Sophie with someone else so I could train with Bryce and Bentley. A lot of strength came with being a shifter, but we still had to exercise to stay in our best shape. And I knew if I ever expected to kill Travis and his mutants I couldn't slack—and that's exactly what I'd been doing.

"So," Evan smirked, "y'all did get married because she was pregnant then."

I shook my head. "No, that happened after, I promise you," I chuckled. I really didn't want to be talking about this with these guys.

I rubbed my hands nervously on my jeans, wishing that a miracle would happen and Sophie would appear so I could disappear from all this awkwardness.

And then, as if conjured by my thoughts alone, I looked out of the family room to see her shakily making her way down the steps.

I hopped up and ran up the steps to her side. Her skin was pale and she was way too frail. This was scaring me more and more with every day that passed. Who would've thought that because we're both Alphas it would complicate the pregnancy? If anything you'd think it'd make it easier.

I placed my arm around her and helped guide her down the steps. She was getting weaker, that much was obvious, and I'd been right before about her losing weight. There was a gaunt hollowness to her cheekbones. It was like the baby was sucking the life right out of her. I didn't know how we were going to make it through this. The baby wasn't due until April. We had a good five more months of this and if she was like this now...I hated to think of what she'd be like by the end of the pregnancy.

"I don't feel good," she admitted reluctantly, looking at me with defeated brown eyes. I knew it was killing her to admit that to me.

"We have visitors," I whispered in her ear.

"Who?" She questioned.

"Your soccer buddies."

Her whole face instantly brightened at that news. Geez, if these guys made her that happy I'd move them in. She spent too much time sulking these days.

"Yeah. Why don't I get you into the family room and bring you some food?" I suggested.

She nodded. "Sounds good, but—uh—I'm in my pajamas."

"That won't do," I eyed her practically see through white t-shirt. I didn't want to let her go, because she looked like she was about to fall over, so I held onto her awkwardly as I shrugged out of my green sweatshirt. I wrapped it around her and helped her get her arms through. I promptly zipped it all the way up. I didn't want any of those guys staring at her.

"Happy now?" She began to laugh but it quickly turned into a cough. Seeing her like this…it felt like I was being stabbed over and over again.

I guided her to the couch and the guys instantly swarmed around her, asking her a million and one questions.

I looked through the pantry for a can of soup. She didn't look like she'd be able to get anything else down. When I found one that didn't sound entirely repulsive, I poured it into a pot to let it heat.

I braced my hands on the counter and my shoulders were tense.

I needed to focus on Travis. I needed to watch the life leave his eyes before our baby came into this world. But Sophie—she was my top priority and until she was well, Travis would have to wait. In life, sacrifices have to be made, and this was one of them.

ELEVEN.
Sophie

"I am *never* having another baby," I seethed, glaring up at Caeden as I slouched over the toilet bowl. "If you ever try to impregnate me again I will cut you."

He didn't laugh at my warning like most guys would have. Instead, his frown deepened further. "I thought the nausea was supposed to go away."

"Maybe if you're a human—" I started to gag and Caeden reached down to pull my hair away from my face. When I had finished retching I began to sob. "I hate this so much. I never thought being pregnant would be like this, Caeden."

He sat down on the bathroom floor and pulled me into his arms. I tried to pull away with protests of my stinky breath, but he wasn't having any of it.

"Stinky or smelling like rainbows, I don't care," he kissed the top of my head.

"Was that supposed to sound romantic? Because it wasn't. Your skills are seriously lacking," I joked.

He chuckled. "Yeah, when you get married you forget how to be charming."

"At least you're mine," I sighed. "I'll keep you anyway, even if you're not charming."

"You love me despite the fact that I'm defective?" He laughed. "Good to know."

We sat on the floor for a few more minutes before he finally coaxed me to stand up. Since I was so weak, he held onto my waist while I brushed my teeth.

"Thank you," I told him as the last of the frothy white goo disappeared down the drain.

He helped me back in the bed and tucked the covers around me. Neither of us had said much about the fact that I was getting weaker every day, but we both knew it. I could see the fear in Caeden's eyes every time he looked at me, and it bothered me that I was the cause.

"I'm going to see Bryce and Bentley," he told me, bending to press a gentle kiss to the top of my head. "Nolan's here so if you need anything, holler for him."

"Okay," I said, even though I hated being left here with Nolan. But Caeden had been leaving more and more. It was obvious he was working out. He was more bulked up now than I'd ever seen him. His shirts had gotten too tight and strained against his muscular chest.

I reached out to touch him, needing to feel him. My hand landed weakly against his chest and he frowned at how prominent my veins had become.

"Everything will be okay," I whispered.

His eyes met mine with disbelief.

"It will. Everything always works out in the end, even if we have to struggle to get there. Think about this, we get to find out if the baby is a boy or girl next Monday. That's exciting, right?"

He nodded, but there was still a shadow clouding his face, and all I wanted to do was chase his storms away.

"I still know it's Lucy," he chuckled. "Call it a father's intuition."

I rolled my eyes. "I say it's Beau."

"It doesn't matter," Caeden smiled, "the baby's going to take after me anyway."

"Whatever," I threw a pillow at him. "Get out of here so you can get home to me sooner."

"I love you," he said as he paused in the doorway.

"Love you too," I smiled at him, waving weakly.

I sighed loudly and both dogs were quick to join me on the bed. I rubbed their heads and it helped to calm me. I knew Caeden had better things to do then sit here with me all day, heck I'd pushed him to leave me alone on many occasions, but I was spending more and more time by myself and to put it bluntly, it sucked.

"I'm sorry, baby," I placed my hand against my stomach. "This may suck, but you're definitely worth it. I can't wait to hold you, baby. Mommy loves you."

Caeden

Bentley spotted me as I lifted the heavy weight above my head. My arms strained and sweat soaked my body, but I didn't care. I didn't even know how much it weighed, but it was heavy, I could tell you that much. I lowered it and lifted it up again, pushing past the burn. My thoughts couldn't wander when I did this. I had to focus entirely on lifting and lowering the weight.

"You should stop," Bentley warned trying to take the weight from me and hook it on the bar.

"No," I growled, tightening my grip.

"You're going to wear yourself out," he taunted, stepping back.

"I. Don't. Care." I huffed between breaths. I saw him shake his head out of my peripheral vision, but he said no more.

I lifted until my arms felt like limp noodles and I couldn't continue. The metal bar clanked loudly and I sat up, my breathing was accelerated and my face was probably red. The muscles in my arms were twitching and burning, but I didn't mind.

"You okay?" Bentley asked.

"Never better," I reached for a towel to dry my damp face.

"Here," he tossed me a bottle of water. "If you're going to go all out you need to keep up your fluids."

I shook my head at his tone. He was worried about me and Bentley was the kind of guy that never worried about anything, so that was saying something.

I guzzled down the bottle of water and held out my hand so he could toss me another one.

I threw the empty bottles in the recycling bin my mom kept in the basement and ran my fingers through my damp hair. "What's up with you?" I asked Bentley. I needed to hear about someone else's life for a change. I was so sick of talking about mine.

He shrugged. "Nothing much to talk about. Chris' is driving me nuts decorating the apartment. She keeps asking me about coordinating colors. Do I *look* like I know anything about coordinating colors?" He shook his head. "I love her anyway, though, even when she's driving me batshit crazy."

"Yeah, they have that effect on you," I shrugged.

"How's Sophie? She didn't look too good when I saw her on Thanksgiving," he asked.

Shit. I didn't avoid talking about my life for long.

"Yeah, she's fine."

Bentley gave me a doubtful look, but didn't push me for more information. That was why we made such good friends. We knew when to leave the other person alone.

"Are you done?" Bentley asked.

I looked around the basement with my hands on my hips. I didn't want to stop, and while being a shifter meant I'd recover quicker than a human from this amount of exertion, I knew I shouldn't push it.

"Nah, I'm done," I tossed the soiled towel into the hamper.

"Want to get something to eat before you head home?"

I thought about it for a moment. "Sure."

I hadn't spent much time with Bentley—any of the pack for that matter—in months. I had my reasons, but I did miss them. There was just so much I couldn't say to them.

Bentley smiled, shaking his dark hair out of his eyes. "That was easier than I thought."

"Yeah, well..."

"'Bout time we had a guys night. Although, you better shower before we do anything. You smell like a five day old tuna sandwich," he pinched his nose in exaggeration.

"I was planning on it," I started towards the showers.

It didn't take me long to wash the sweat and grime from my skin. Since I'd been spending so much time here, I also had a stash of clean clothes. I sent Sophie a text letting her know I'd be later than I planned. I held my breath for a reply and sighed in relief when she said okay.

It would've worried me if I hadn't heard from her and Bentley would have ended up wanting to punch me.

"Ready?" Bentley asked me as I tugged my shirt down.

"Yeah," I nodded, my stomach already rumbling.

We each took separate cars and met at the restaurant. It was loud in there and to my sensitive ears it was a killer.

"You couldn't have picked somewhere else to eat?" I questioned Bentley. "I think my eardrums are going to burst."

"Hey, I wanted the green bean fries, those things are delicious. *And* you did tell me I could pick the place," he continued to scan the menu. "So quit your complaining."

He had a point.

A waitress appeared and we placed our order. We both got cheeseburgers and two orders of Bentley's beloved green bean fries—which sounded gross to me, but he said I'd end up hogging them, hence the two orders.

We chatted about random things. *Human* things. It was nice to be a normal guy for a change, even if it was only for a night.

By the time we left the restaurant we were laughing and carrying on like we'd drunk a couple of beers, but neither of us had actually had anything to drink.

"We have to do this again soon," Bentley thumped my back as he passed me on the way to his car. "I need more guy time, and less estrogen."

I nodded in agreement. I needed to be better at finding *balance*. That had always been my problem. I went all out, and I forgot to *breathe*. I scrubbed my hand over my face before I started the car.

I decided to make a pit stop on my way home and got ice cream and toppings so we could make our own sundaes. It wasn't much, but I thought Sophie would enjoy it.

I'd been gone all day and the house was dark and quiet. I hoped Nolan hadn't left. I hated to think of Sophie here by herself all that time, but I knew if she had really needed me she would have called.

I grabbed two bowls out of the cabinet and made our sundaes. They weren't the prettiest things ever created, but we were only going to eat them so I didn't see how it mattered.

I carried the bowls upstairs and kicked open the bedroom door.

"I'm not hungry," were the first words out of Sophie's mouth.

"Good, because this isn't food. It's ice cream. Big difference," I grinned.

She instantly brightened and a huge smile spread across her pretty face. God, I loved that smile, I lived for it actually.

"Ice cream? I haven't had ice cream in forever," she pushed herself up and adjusted the pillows behind her back before holding out her hands for a bowl.

I handed it to her and changed into my jammie jams—I couldn't ever seem to call them pajamas—before climbing into bed beside her.

"This is so yummy," she moaned, licking the spoon. "You even put sprinkles and whipped cream on it...ooh, is that a brownie mixed in?"

I laughed at her excitement. It didn't take much to make my girl happy, all the more reason to love her.

"It most certainly is."

"You, are without a doubt, the greatest husband to ever walk the planet," she beamed.

"Wow, that's a high honor. If I knew ice cream was the way too your heart I would've gotten you some a long time ago," I chuckled, taking a bite of my own ice cream. I had opted for plain vanilla loaded with a half a bottle's worth of chocolate syrup. Sophie's was vanilla ice cream with chocolate syrup, brownie bits, sprinkles, whipped cream, and a cherry on top of course.

She smacked my arm in jest and it worried me how weak the force behind the touch had been. She wasn't well and I didn't know what to do to make it better. Lucinda wasn't a doctor, and Sophie's real doctor was a human, so it wasn't like we could explain the situation to him. He'd think we were crazy.

"What are you thinking about?" Sophie asked.

"Nothing important," I leaned over and kissed her cheek, before taking another bite of ice cream.

"Ew," she wiped her cheek on her shirt sleeve, "you got syrup on my face, and now it's all sticky."

"Sticky with my love," I taunted.

"You're disgusting."

"You love me, so I don't know what that says about you," I shrugged.

"It says I have horrible taste," her lips quirked up in a small smile.

It was nice to sit and joke for a change. The dark heavy cloud that had been hanging over us for way too long was still there, but right now there was a small glimmer of sunshine and we both needed to bask in its glow.

"That hurts, Sophie. It really hurts."

She rolled her eyes and licked ice cream off her lips. "Thanks for this," she said after a moment. "I...I needed this."

"I did too."

When our bowls were empty I took them to the kitchen to wash them. By the time I made it back to the room Sophie was asleep, both the dogs curled up beside her, and there was whipped cream dried above her top lip, creating an adorable mustache.

I turned the light off and climbed in beside her. The dogs got disgruntled and jumped off the bed. Sophie let off a soft cry at the disruption and then rolled over, curling her body into mine. I inhaled her sweet scent of cookies and gathered her into my arms. She rubbed her face against my chest and made a cute little sleepy sound. Her round stomach pressed up against me and I marveled at it. It seemed like overnight her stomach had went from flat to a bump. She was the most beautiful pregnant woman I'd ever seen—not that I was biased or anything.

"I wuv you," she murmured in her sleep.

I chuckled.

She'd been doing that a lot lately—talking in her sleep. She said some pretty funny things too. One time she said, "Don't take my salad!" Um, okay, I won't take your salad you weirdo. I really wondered what she'd been dreaming to say *that* in her sleep. *I wuv you*, was self-explanatory.

I smoothed my hand over her cheekbone, marveling at the softness of her cheek. Her lips pouted in her sleep and her nose scrunched. She curled her head under my neck and her ear rested against where my heart beat steadily in my chest.

I kissed the top of her head and then her forehead. I loved her with every fiber of my being and I'd never stop…not just because we were mates, but because she was *Sophie*.

TWELVE.
Sophie

I took a deep breath, preparing myself for the most monumental news of my life. I knew I didn't care whether the baby was a boy or girl, but once I knew it would make it even more real.

I would be able to picture him or her even more clearly in my mind.

"You've lost weight," the doctor said when I stepped off the scale. "Hop up here and let's check on your baby." Worry incased his words, which in turn made me worry like a crazy person. I'd never forgive myself if something happened to my baby.

Fear shimmered in Caeden's eyes when I met his gaze. There was so much we couldn't tell my doctor, and unfortunately, none of the shifters in our pack had studied to be a doctor.

I closed my eyes and draped my arm over my face. I waited with bated breath to hear the sound of our baby's heartbeat. But…but what if it never came?

It would devastate me. That was for sure.

Then, I heard it. Strong and steady the baby's heartbeat echoed through the room. All three of us let out a sigh of relief and I lowered my arm, opening my eyes.

"Is the baby okay?" I questioned breathlessly.

"Give me one minute," he flicked a couple things and moved the wand around. "The baby is the right size, heartbeat is excellent, and it's moving around like I want to see. Are you feeling any movement?"

"Not really." I frowned. "Is that a bad thing?"

"Not at all. You might not feel any movement for another week or so. Or you might be feeling it now and attributing it to something else. I do want you to amp up on your vitamin intake. The weight loss isn't affecting the baby—yet—but it is affecting you. We want you to be as healthy as possible for you and the baby. Understand?"

I nodded.

"Now," he looked between Caeden and me, "are you ready to find out the sex?"

"Yes," I nodded enthusiastically, as my heart raced in my chest like it was going to fall out and flop on the floor.

Caeden reached for my hand and we both held our breath as we waited for the doctor to tell us if we were about to welcome a daughter or son.

He moved the wand lower over my stomach and said, "Congrats, it's a boy. You're going to have a son."

I promptly burst into tears—and not the cute dainty tears most girls had, I'm talking full on ugly crying. I was going to have a *son*—a little boy to hold in my arms and to love forever.

"Beau," I whispered *his* name as love flowed through my veins. I'd loved the baby before now, but knowing that it was a boy and saying his name, made it *real*.

I wiped my tears away and began to laugh, embarrassed by my reaction. But then I looked at Caeden and saw a tear snaking its way down his cheek and it didn't make me feel crazy.

"Baby Beau," he whispered. "I'm going to have a son…" He wiped the single tear away and shook his head. "Wow."

The doctor handed us the sonogram pictures and we headed on our way. We were both quiet in the car, lost in our thoughts.

Just as Caeden pulled into the garage, he turned to me. "When are we going to tell our parents?"

"I don't know," I picked at a worn thread on my jeans. "Maybe we should tell them on Christmas, so they all find out together."

Christmas was only two weeks away, and while that seemed like forever to wait, I knew it would be fun to surprise them.

Caeden thought over what I said and nodded. "That's a good idea. They'll like that."

"Maybe we can get three pairs of little blue socks and wrap them."

He leaned over and pressed a kiss to my lips. "Whatever you want," his fingers skimmed lightly over cheek and down my chin. I knew he was trying to appease me since I'd lost so much freedom the last five months, but instead of getting mad, I smiled in appreciation. I was really lucky to have him. He understood me and knew when he'd pushed me too far. He'd done really well about not being nearly as overprotective and he'd been spending more time doing other things. I was happy that he was getting out and not exiling himself along with me.

* * *

Bryce, Nolan, Gram, my mom and dad, Amy, and Caeden gathered in the family room. Christmas music played and the tree was all lit up and overflowing with decorations. I'd baked chocolate chip cookies this morning for everyone. Bryce looked like he'd already scarfed down about ten.

"Cold?" Gram asked me.

"Huh?"

"You have on this huge sweater. You must be cold," she commented.

"Oh, uh, yeah," I nodded. "I'm cold." I was cold almost all the time now, but that wasn't the reason for the sweater. I'd chosen the large clunky sweater to hide how small my frame had become. I'd had to use makeup to hide the dark circles under my eyes and the gauntness of my cheekbones.

Gram eyed me for a moment, not believing it, and then moved further into the room to sit on the couch.

I let out a sigh of relief that I'd dodged that bullet.

I sat beside Caeden on the floor by the tree and he draped a blanket over my shoulders. A fire roared in the fireplace and everything was just so…perfect. It was everything I could ever hope to ask for, but there was so much going on behind the scenes that none of them knew about.

"When are we going to open presents?" Bryce whined. I swear, you'd think he was seven, not seventeen.

"Right now, doucheknozzle," Caeden grabbed a package and threw it at his brother.

Bryce caught it and checked the nametag. "This is for Sophie," he tossed it back. "If you're going to throw a present at my head, make sure it's one for me first."

Caeden rolled his eyes, grabbed another present, which he checked the label on, and threw it with more force at Bryce. The box blurred as it flew threw the air and smacked Bryce on the forehead. Luckily, his curls seemed to have softened the blow.

"That. Was. Not. Nice." Bryce glared. "But since this one's actually for me, I won't complain…too much."

He promptly began ripping the wrapping paper off, throwing it everywhere, some even landed in his hair.

"Look's like this one's for you," Caeden handed me the small box he'd previously tossed at Bryce. It was wrapped carefully in shiny green paper with a small red bow. The box was small and shaking it only produced a quiet rustling sound, which was unhelpful in identifying what the item was. "Open it," he coaxed with a small boyish smile.

I slowly unfurled the paper, and a small white box sat in the palm of my hand. I lifted the lid off and was greeted by the sight of a bracelet. I picked it up, looking it over. The band was made of some kind of rubbery mint green material and it connected to an infinity symbol.

"I know you already have this one," he flicked the bracelet he'd made me last year for Christmas that never left my wrist. "But I felt like making another."

"You made this one too?" I questioned, gazing at him with wide eyes as I slipped the bracelet onto my wrist.

He nodded. "Yes," he whispered huskily in my ear, sending a shiver down my spine, "because you and me, we're for infinity."

God, I loved the sound of that. Caeden had always had an unfair way with words. I was never able to express my feelings as beautifully as he could. "Thank you," I said simply, rubbing my finger over the infinity symbol.

He kissed the top of my head, his lips lingering against my skin longer than necessary. "You're welcome."

More presents were unwrapped and we finally handed Gram, Amy, and my parents their separate boxes. My heart thundered in my chest with nerves. I knew none of them cared if the baby was a boy or girl, but it was exciting telling them. I really hoped my dad didn't cry again. Growing up, I had *never* seen the man cry, but apparently a grandchild made the man all weepy.

Caeden sat back and pulled me into the V of his legs. He rubbed his hands soothingly up and down my arms to calm me. It wasn't necessary, but I liked the feel of his hands on me, so I didn't complain.

I watched as they all held the pale blue matching sets of socks and hats and the realization hit them.

"A boy? You're having a boy?" Amy beamed, clutching the small items tightly in her hands like we might snatch them away at any second.

"We're having a son," Caeden confirmed as he pressed his lips against my cheek.

"Do you have a name picked out?" My mom asked. "Or have you not decided yet?"

"Do you want to tell them?" Caeden whispered in my ear.

I nodded. Looking at my dad, I placed my hand against my stomach, "We're naming him Beaumont, but calling him Beau."

"That's—that's—thank you," he blubbered. "That means a lot. I'm glad the Beaumont name is carrying on in some way."

"What about a middle name?" Amy asked.

I shrugged. "We haven't talked about that. But Beaumont Williams seems like such a big name already, does he really need a middle name too?"

"That's true," Amy agreed. "Beau is a great name."

"I think so too," I smiled up at Caeden. Love reflected back to me from his eyes—a love that not many people experienced—the selfless kind.

After all the presents were unwrapped, we cleaned up the mess of paper...or tried to. Bryce kept making a bigger mess. Sometimes I swore the guy was still five years old. He might have been a goof, but I knew his sense of humor probably camouflaged his demons.

The evening past quickly and Amy made a delicious dinner while Gram baked cupcakes. I hadn't had one of her cupcakes in so long and ended up eating four before Caeden could stop me.

Sitting around the roaring fire with my whole family made me so incredibly happy. This was the stuff dreams were made of—only I was living it.

THIRTEEN.
Sophie

I stood in the middle of the room that would soon be Beau's. Painters rolled a beige color onto the walls since we'd opted not to go with the traditional pale blue.

I couldn't believe that in a few months, my son would be in this room.

"Soph!" Caeden cried, running into the room and grabbing my arm. "You shouldn't be in here! The paint fumes!"

"You worry too much," I sighed. "They're using that non-toxic paint, so quit freaking out. It's annoying."

"I still don't think you should be in here," he slowly began to drag me out of the room.

Wanting to avoid an argument, I let him.

"I talked to Chris," I told him, letting him guide me back to the bedroom. I was weak, but I wasn't *that* weak. I was perfectly capable of walking on my own without falling, but Caeden believed otherwise. I think he invented stuff to worry about. In fact, I was feeling better these last few weeks. Christmas with our family had given me a much needed boost...or maybe it was the cupcakes. Those had been awfully yummy.

"Why is that important?" He asked.

"Because, she's taking me shopping for baby stuff."

"No, no way, not happening," he rapidly shook his head as he released his hold on me. "You're too weak to go shopping. Remember what happened last time? And that was months ago!"

"Caeden, I don't care how weak I am, you're not stopping me from going shopping for the baby. *Nothing* about this pregnancy has gone as expected, let me have some fun!"

He sighed, running his fingers through his too long hair. He knew there was no stopping me. He wasn't my prison guard and he had no right to *forbid* me to go anywhere.

"Chris may not know the whole story, but she does know I haven't felt well. She'll look out for me," I continued, slowly breaking down his walls so we could avoid a fight. "And you know I'd *never* do anything to jeopardize Beau. If I start to feel like it's too much, I'll tell Chris to bring me home."

His resolve crumbled and I knew I'd be able to leave without an argument.

"Have fun," he grabbed me by the nape of the neck and kissed me tenderly. "If you get too weak or feel any twinge of pain, *come home*," he tucked a piece of hair behind my ear.

"You know I will," I placed my hands on his chest, grasping the soft fabric of his shirt between my fingers.

He took a deep breath, wrapping me tighter in his arms. "Maybe I could go—"

"No," I dug a finger into his ribs, "this is my girl's day. Stay here and hang out with Nolan. Or go out and do something."

"I just have a bad feeling about this…what if you pass out, Soph?"

"I won't be alone, you know that. I know you're worried about me, heck, I'm worried about myself! But I can't stop *living*. The doctor says Beau is fine."

"But *you* are not fine," he countered.

"You already told me to have fun," I smiled up at him. "Now stop trying to talk me out of going. It's not working."

He cracked a small smile. "There's my she-wolf. I've missed her."

"Yeah, well," I put a hand to my stomach, "she's turned into an exhausted incubator."

That got a genuine laugh out of him. "At least you're a cute incubator."

"Mhmm, nice try," I laughed. My phone buzzed in my pocket and I knew that meant Chris was here. "I have to go."

"What if I want to keep you?" He whispered huskily, lightly brushing his lips over mine.

"Are you trying to bribe me with your kisses, Caeden?"

"They're very good kisses." His tongue flicked against my slightly parted lips and my eyes fluttered closed at the touch.

"Nice try." I managed to find the strength to push myself away from his very alluring lips.

"Have fun," he repeated, "I mean it."

Before I could reply, he grabbed me by the waist and pulled me into him. My baby bump kept quite a bit of distance between us, but it didn't stop him from kissing me deeply. It was the kind of kiss that made your toes curl and your heart swell. "I love you," he whispered when he stepped back.

"I love you too," I replied, trying not to sway with lightheadedness.

"Oh," he grabbed my arm to halt me before I could pass him. "Do me a favor?"

"Sure."

"Don't buy a crib," he stated.

"Uh...I'm confused," I stammered. "Why don't you want me to buy a crib?"

"Because," he grinned crookedly, "I'm going to make one for the baby."

"A crib? You're going to make a crib? Like build one?"

"I think that was implied," he laughed.

"That's...sweet." Oh, God. I was tearing up. I really hated these pregnancy hormones.

"Aw, Soph, don't cry," he frowned.

"I'm fine," I hastily shook my head. "I think that's great, Caeden."

"Glad you approve," he grinned.

My phone buzzed in my pocket again and I knew Chris was getting pissy with me.

"I'll be back in two hours," I kissed his cheek and slowly made my way downstairs. I pushed the button to open the gate and pulled on my jacket, a hat, scarf, and gloves. No way was I freezing death.

Chris was waiting outside in her blue Nissan Juke. I thought the small vehicle looked like a bug, but she loved the thing.

We headed into the city, chatting along the way. She was having fun decorating her and Bentley's new place and adjusting to married life. Those two were so cute together and I was beyond happy for them. They deserved their happily ever after.

"We can't dawdle, as much as I'd like to, or Caeden will hunt us down," I warned Chris when we arrived at the mall.

"Why?" She asked, turned the car off and brushing her blonde hair from her eyes.

Oh, crap.

"Um, you know, since I'm getting sick all the time," I stammered. It wasn't a lie.

She was quiet—unusual for Chris—and finally she nodded.

Snow flurries started falling and I was thankful for my multiple layers as we scurried into the entrance. All the baby clothes immediately distracted me, and Chris was just as enthralled.

"They're so tiny," she held up a little dress. "Look how wittle."

"Did you seriously just say 'wittle?'" I questioned, fighting a laugh.

"I did."

I picked up a pale blue blanket with white dots on it and rubbed the soft material between my fingers.

"Are you having a boy?" Chris asked.

"Yeah, a boy. His name is Beau," I smiled at her. I felt bad though that I hadn't told her sooner. Being trapped inside the house had caused me to completely forget that my friends still existed.

"I can't believe you're having a baby," she smiled wistfully. "It's just…"

"Weird?" I supplied. "Believe me, I know," I flicked through a rack of clothes. "I never expected my life to turn out like this. Not that I'm complaining, or anything. Despite all the bad, I have so much to be thankful for."

"And you might just have spoken too soon."

My eyes widened in shock and my movements ceased as I heard those words—and they didn't come from Chris.

My heart galloped in my chest and I broke out in a sweat.

"Hello, Travis," I gasped.

Fear snaked down my spine as I felt his body press into mine. Where the heck had Chris gone?

"If you're looking for your…*friend*," he sneered the word like it was dirty, "you'll find that she's indisposed at the moment."

I swallowed thickly, my eyes scanning for her blonde hair. I gasped when I saw her lying on the mall floor, blood trickling out of her skull.

"She's not dead," his fingers brushed over my forehead. "I have no interest in killing her."

"But you want to kill me," I stated.

"Now, now, my dear Sophie, I wouldn't go as far as to say that," his cold fingers tangled in my hair. I opened my mouth to scream and he promptly slammed a hand against my mouth to silence me. My eyes flickered around, praying someone saw what was happening, but there was no one in sight. "If you scream, I can promise you'll regret it *very* much." He punctuated his threat by pressing a knife into my side.

I closed my eyes, breathing heavily. I was stuck in a very sticky situation here and I didn't see what else I could do besides comply with his wishes. I couldn't shift, and I was too weak to fight him. I had to do what was best for my baby, and unfortunately, at this moment, that meant listening to Travis.

When he felt my body relax, he lowered his hand from my mouth, but the knife pressed harder into my side, piercing the fabric of my jacket. "What do you want?"

"You."

FOURTEEN.
Sophie

You.

You.

You.

The word kept echoing around my skull like a bouncing Ping-Pong ball.

You.

You.

You.

There was a throbbing in my head and I was surrounded by darkness.

Or maybe my eyes were just closed.

Yeah, that was it.

It felt like they were glued shut.

I tried to lift my arms to rub them, but found myself unable to move.

My heart thundered in my chest and my breath echoed around me.

You.

You.

You.

Travis.

Oh my God, Travis had me.

After he said, 'you,' everything went black. Nothing. Nada.

And I still couldn't get my eyes to open!

Panic was crawling through my body, leaving iciness in its wake.

It had all been leading to this.

Every single moment had been building to my death.

From the very beginning Travis was supposed to kill me.

It didn't happen before, so it was happening now.

* * *

"They've been gone for four hours!" I paced the length of the kitchen while Nolan watched me.

"They probably got distracted by makeup…or purses. Isn't that what chicks like?" He tried to be the voice of reason, but I was beyond *reason.*

"Sophie knows she shouldn't be gone that long, and she'd call me if they decided to stay longer," I pulled at my hair. I knew I was acting like a crazy person, but my gut was telling me something bad had happened. I *hoped* I was being paranoid, but I didn't believe that was the case. I left the kitchen to look out the front windows, praying I'd see Christian's car pull up to the gate—which I could just barely see. But there was nothing.

"Why don't you call her?" Nolan stepped up behind me.

"You know I tried that," I growled, my fists clenching at my sides. I was about three seconds away from punching him in the face. "I even called Christian and neither one of them answers. It's not normal. Maybe Bentley's heard from them," I rambled, reaching for my phone in my pocket.

"Wait," Nolan grabbed my arm, halting my movements.

"Let. Me. Go." I was so gonna snap his neck.

"I'm serious, Caeden. You and Sophie are mates, which means you should be able to track her."

I sighed. "I haven't been able to feel her since she got pregnant. It's like our connection is disrupted because of the baby's strength."

Nolan stepped back, shaking his head. "Call Bentley then."

I fumbled with my phone—my fingers unusually clumsy—but I finally managed to get the call to go through.

"Hey, what's up?" Bentley answered.

"Have you heard from Christian?"

"Uh…no. I figured she was at your house, hanging out with Sophie after shopping."

"Well, they're not here," I growled, pacing again. I was going to wear a hole right through the floor if I kept this up.

"And they haven't called?" I heard panic begin to lace Bentley's words.

"No," I stopped in front of the window beside the door once more. "Wait, I see Chris' car right now," I sighed in relief. They were okay. *Sophie* was okay.

"Thank God," Bentley said before I hung up the phone. I ran to the garage door and punched the button to open the gate. I waited outside, snow melting on my heated bare skin.

The car raced up the driveway and came to a screeching halt in front of me. Christian all but fell out of the car and I raced to her side to keep her from falling. Her skin was abnormally pale and her eyes flitted around, as if expecting someone to jump out at us.

"What is it, Christian?" I asked, trying to peer around her to see Sophie.

"I'm so sorry, Caeden," she sobbed. "He came up behind me and—and—" she sobbed. "Everything went dark and when I woke up, she was gone."

"Who was gone?" I growled, needing to hear her say it.

"Sophie. She's gone, Caeden. He has her. Travis has her." Her tears splashed onto my skin.

I sank to the ground, Christian falling with me. A sound that wasn't even remotely human escaped my throat.

Sophie.

He has Sophie.

He has my she-wolf.

My wife.

My baby.

My *life*.

Travis had it all now.

I took deep breaths, my vision blurring. My nails began to lengthen and my neck stretched. I hadn't had an uncontrolled shift since I was sixteen, but right now, I was really close to losing it.

Out of the corner of my eye, I saw Nolan emerge from the open garage door.

"She's gone. She's gone. She's gone," I repeated over and over again. Even when my teeth started to lengthen, I kept saying it.

I fought the shift as much as I could, but it became too much, and my wolf skin burst free.

I felt like someone had ripped my heart out and stomped on it repeatedly.

I tilted my head back and howled at the sky above me.

Every single pack member—even the elders—would be unable to resist the call of their Alpha. I might not have trusted the elders right now, but I needed to see them. I needed to look them in the eye and watch for a reaction. I needed to find out where Sophie was, and I was sure one of them—either Cody, Charlotte's grandpa, or Baxter, Bentley's grandpa—knew where she was. I didn't care if they were our *elders* or my friends' grandparents, I'd rip them apart and watch the life drain from their eyes if I believed for even one second that they were responsible for Sophie being taken…and not just that, but *everything* that had happened since my dad was murdered. I wasn't going to sit back and be passive. I would start a war if that's what it took to get my she-wolf back. She was worth everything, and if they didn't understand that, then they better watch their backs.

FIFTEEN.
Sophie

I had passed out again. But now I was wide awake, staring at a plain white ceiling, with my hands strapped tightly to the headboard of the bed I was lying in. The room wasn't anything special. The walls were beige and the furniture was white. There was a window, but it was covered with curtains so I couldn't tell whether it was day or night. I wondered how much time had passed since I'd been taken. Hours? Days?

I yanked my arms forward, rattling the chains wrapped around my wrists. I was literally tied up like I was some kind of animal.

My body was tired and so I knew I didn't stand a chance of escape. I was trapped.

I rattled the chains again, letting out a scream.

How had this happened?

I was terrified as I scrolled through the different reasons why Travis would be keeping me here. Wherever *here* was. I wasn't really scared for myself though. No, all my worries for my baby.

The door eased open and I pulled harder against the chains, like I could break them with sheer willpower alone. Travis stuck his head through the doorway and smiled when he saw that I was awake. My heart beat rapidly in my chest as envisioned him shoving a knife through my heart or cutting me into little bitty pieces to feed to his mutants.

"I'm happy to see you're awake." His voice was oddly pleasant. I was used to an angry and crazy Travis...not one that was so calm. I think I preferred psychotic Travis to this one. There was something creepy about how...peaceful he acted. He paraded about the room, continuing to talk. He acted as if this was an every day occurrence, like I *lived* here, and wasn't chained to a bed like an animal.

122

I watched his lips move as he spoke, but it was like my ears had stopped working because I didn't hear a thing he said. I was oddly detached, waiting for the moment when he would strike and my life—and my child's—would end. I knew in my heart that my death was inevitable, and so I wished he'd just do it instead of dragging it out.

He continued to walk the length of the room and finally stopped beside me. He reached out, and I flinched, unable to control my reaction. He made a hushing sound, like I was a frightened animal he was trying to console. What the heck? This was getting weirder and weirder. Maybe I was dreaming…no, this was far to real to be a dream.

"Do you like the room?"

What? I couldn't have heard him right.

"Do you like the room?" He repeated, staring at me with eyes dark as night.

"Huh?" I blinked my eyes rapidly. Surely I was imagining this. There was no way Travis was asking me if I liked the freakin' room!

"The room," he waved his hand, encompassing the space, "do you like it?"

"Are you crazy?!" I screeched, pulling against the chains binding me once more. My wrist burned where the metal dug into my skin. "You have me *trapped* here."

"Trapped is such a harsh word," he reached out, stroking my cheek with the back of his hand. "You'll be happy here…one day."

"What are you talking about?" I panted, gritting my teeth as I strained away from his touch.

"We're going to be a family."

Nothing, and I do mean *nothing*, could have prepared me to hear those words leave Travis' lips.

We're going to be a family.

We. As in me, Travis, and my baby.

He really was off his rocker. I'd slit his throat with my very human fingernails before I let that happen.

"We are *not* a family," I spat, still trying to get away from him. I was tempted to cry from the pain radiating in my arms from having my hands chained above my head.

"You may think that now," his fingers lingered on my lips, "but you'll change your mind."

"I'll never change my mind," I growled, my heart racing in my chest as his hand ventured over the curve of my breasts. I cringed, bile rising in my throat. The dude was my *cousin*.

"I can be very persuasive," he smirked, his eyes flashing gold before returning to black.

I opened my mouth to respond, but his hand slapped my cheek. The skin stung like a bitch and I was sure it was an angry red. Tears I couldn't control filled my eyes.

I glared at Travis. "What the hell was that for?"

"You need to learn manners," he lowered so we were eye to eye. "Caeden might like your smart mouth, but I won't stand for it. You're mine now, sweet Sophie," he smoothed his fingers over my throbbing cheek in a gentle touch.

His mouth lowered on mine, and on instinct I bit down on his lip.

He jumped back and I saw a small trickle of blood.

Anger contorted his features. He reached out, grabbing a chunk of my hair, and pulled.

A scream tore out of my throat. Not only was it extremely painful having your hair ripped from your skull, but he pulled me against the chains. I heard a pop and I'm pretty sure my shoulder dislocated.

"Manners," he pointed a finger in my face. "I expect you to have learned some when I return, and if you haven't, *this* will seem like nothing," he shoved his hand in front of me that contained long strands of my dark hair.

He turned sharply on his heel and stormed out of the room. The door slammed closed behind him and it sounded like he locked a deadbolt.

I began to cry.

I was never going to make it out of here alive.

124

I'd already come to that conclusion before. But now, being awake, seeing Travis…it had really hit me.

I was going to die, and there was nothing I could do about it, but that didn't mean I'd go down without a fight. I had my baby, and Caeden, to think about. I was a mama wolf now, and we weren't to be trifled with. If Travis thought he'd be able to *break* me, he was *wrong.*

* * *

Caeden

I wanted to kill all of them.

Every single one of them.

Even my friends.

I'm sure that made me like Travis, but right now I didn't give a crap.

Sophie was gone, and they were looking at me like I was out of my mind. I wanted them to pay, because I knew one of them had to be a mole. Maybe even more than one. Power was a sticky fickle thing, and it got to the best of them. And Travis, with his mutants, had a lot of power.

Everyone was gathered outside, I was too angry to ask them in, and frankly I didn't want a *traitor* in my house.

I was beyond keeping my beliefs to myself anymore. I wanted everyone to know.

"There's a traitor among us," I stated, and gasps abounded. "And I promise you, when I find out who it is," I glared at everyone, lingering on Cody and Baxter, "there will be hell to pay."

I watched as everyone looked around, eyeing each other as whispers spread.

"I don't know why you're so mad about Sophie being gone," Cody eyed me. "You're mates, surely you can feel her."

I couldn't control my reaction. I grabbed him by the collar and lifted the older man high into the air. "I *can't* feel her, because of the *baby*. I'm not as stupid as you think, Cody," I dropped the man, but he landed on his feet.

"Grandpa!" Charlotte rushed to Cody's side.

"Caeden, you need to calm down," Bryce grabbed my arm, trying to pull me away.

I slung his hold off with so much force that he went flying through the air and landed on his butt.

Anger coursed through my veins like a powerful drug. For the first time in my whole life, I hated what I was. Being a shifter had caused this. I might lose everything to that psycho because I belonged to this world.

I crumpled to my knees as defeat hit me.

A cry escaped my throat and I grasped at the snow, letting the cold seep into me, reminding me that I was alive. Alive, while Sophie was either dead, or fighting for her life. I'd never forgive myself for this, and I wouldn't be surprised if she hated me if—no, *when*—I found her. Because I would find her…and she'd be alive.

I had to believe that, or I couldn't keep going.

I finally rose, bracing my shoulders against the cold wind. "I want you all gone," I whispered, knowing they'd hear me. When none of them moved, my anger returned. "LEAVE!"

I watched as they began to shift back to their wolf form and left. Bentley, Christian, my mom, Bryce, Sophie's parents, and Lucinda lingered.

"Go away!" I yelled at them, not caring how harsh I sounded.

No one moved though.

They stared at me, watching as I broke apart. I was their Alpha and they shouldn't see me like this. But today's events had taken its toll on me. I'd lost Sophie and threatened my pack—which went against everything an Alpha stood for. You were a leader, the voice of reason, you weren't supposed to threaten your pack. But I meant every word. I wasn't going to be weak and stand by. It was probably a bad thing that I'd let my belief of a mole be known, but I'd needed to say it. I couldn't keep everything bottled inside anymore.

As my family and friends stood, watching me, I finally got the strength to stand once more.

Garrett, Sophie's dad, was the first to approach me.
"We're going to get her back."
I nodded, but I wasn't so sure.

SIXTEEN.

Eight days.

One hundred and ninety-two hours.

Eleven thousand five hundred and twenty minutes.

Six hundred ninety-two thousand and two hundred seconds.

That was how long Sophie had been gone.

How was it possible that I continued to live and function without my heart and soul?

I wasn't sleeping.

I wasn't eating.

I was existing.

Going through the motions with no destination.

I was half out of my mind and there was nothing I could do to change it. Sophie was gone, and I couldn't find her. I'd been searching and searching, and always came up empty. I was tempted to rip out Cody and Baxter's throats just to feel like I was doing something.

I'd never been a violent person, but losing Sophie again was making me more animal than man. Being separated from your mate was a painful thing and I wasn't even experiencing those affects because the baby disrupted our connection. Despite that, I *knew* she wasn't dead. I'd feel it if…if he killed her. I almost threw up at the very thought. I hoped, wherever she was, that she knew I'd find her.

* * *

Sophie

My whole body hurt like I'd been run over by a car…actually a train seemed more accurate.

I wouldn't summit to Travis' delusion that we were going to be a family, so he hit me. A lot.

I was close to giving in though.

Not because I was hurting—even though I was—and not because I'd given up. I could take anything he dealt me. But I was concerned about the baby. He moved inside me restlessly and it was like he was aware that we were in danger. I couldn't keep letting Travis hurt me, because it hurt Beau.

I had resolved that when he returned to the room I was confined in, I'd play into his fantasy. I wasn't an actress, but when you're in a life or death situation, the things you can do are pretty remarkable.

I sat up, which was difficult with my arms chained above my head, and licked my parched lips. It had been a while since Travis had visited me, and he hadn't brought water or food with him then. I think his new tactic, instead of violence, was to starve me until I caved to his demands. Little did he know that I was already there.

"Mommy's going to protect you," I whispered to my bump. Talking to the baby was the only thing keeping me sane.

I took a deep breath and started counting the cracks and dents in the ceiling. It was the only thing I had to do that passed the time. Boredom was a killer. And while counting wasn't fun, it was something.

Maybe if I was nice to Travis he'd let me have a TV.

I wondered if I could sweet-talk him into unchaining me? I didn't think any amount of eyelash batting on my part would get him to let me leave this room, but if I got unchained at least my arms would have relief and I'd be free to move about.

I sighed loudly, my breath the only sound in the room except for the steady humming of the heater.

My arms and wrists had long since gone numb, and the pain from my dislocated shoulder was just a dull throb now.

I closed my eyes, taking deep breaths.

I felt like I'd been here forever, and I wondered how long I could possibly survive this. I knew Caeden would be looking for me, but he couldn't just storm in here and take me back. I knew from the sounds I heard outside my door, that there were way more people here than Travis, and I was sure they were his mutants. I shuddered at the thought of him unleashing one of those things on me. I still couldn't get the image out of my head of the one that killed Logan. I knew that was something that would haunt me for the rest of my life—whether my life ended soon or I managed to live to be old and gray.

My eyes popped open as I heard shuffling footsteps outside my door. I swallowed thickly, hearing the click of the deadbolt and then watching the knob turn slowly. So far, Travis had been the only person to 'visit' me, but I still feared that he might send one of his mutants in here to finish me off.

The door opened completely and Travis stood with a tray of food. "Morning, sunshine," he grinned, kicking the heavy door closed behind him.

He laid the tray across my lap and sat on the foot of the bed. "Eat up. I know you must be hungry."

And you must be crazy.

"I can't move my arms." I shook the chains for emphasis.

"Oh, of course, I forgot."

He moved and I dared to hope he was going to unchain me. He scooted closer and grabbed a piece of toast covered in butter off the plate. "Here," he held it to my lips.

I fought tears. He wasn't going to unchain me. There was no telling how long he'd leave me like this.

I hesitated before taking a bite, thinking for a moment that it was possible that he'd poisoned it. But that wasn't Travis' style. He preferred to spill your blood and guts everywhere.

I opened my mouth, tearing off a piece of the bread and chewing slowly.

"Good girl," he crooned and I half expected him to do something silly like pet my head.

I took another bite, my stomach churning with the sudden intake of food. I'd have to be careful or I'd make myself sick if I ate too much.

I finished the half slice of toast and he held a glass of water to my lips. I greedily swallowed down the cool liquid.

He held the other slice of toast up to my lips and I ate it slowly. Never, in a million years, would I have guessed that I'd have Travis hand feeding me. True, he'd kidnapped me, but he'd never been compassionate. You'd think he wouldn't care if I starved to death.

I finished the toast and water and Travis removed the tray from my lap. I expected him to leave, but he didn't. He left the tray by the door and returned to sit on the end of the bed.

"I left for a while to give you time to think," his hand skated up my calf, stopping at my knee, and I tried not to shudder. Thank goodness I at least had a blanket covering my legs. "I hope, now, that you've come to appreciate what I've given you." His gaze flicked around them room before those black, lifeless, eyes landed on me again.

I swallowed thickly, preparing myself to lie. "I have."

It was only two words, two words I'd barely been able to whisper, but Travis smiled from ear to ear. I don't think I'd ever seen him smile. He wasn't as scary, and seemed more human. But the smile didn't fool me. Travis was a killer, and the minute I didn't play along with his game he wouldn't hesitate to slit my throat.

"Good," he patted my knee affectionately. He leaned close to me, his face only centimeters from mine. I held my breath, not wanting to inhale the same air he was breathing. "I have a reward for you."

A-a reward?" I stuttered.

"Mhmm," he hummed as he stood. He reached above my head and undid the binding on my hands. My arms flopped to my sides, the muscles feeling dead. I could feel the blood flowing through my veins trying to bring life back to the limbs.

Before I could rejoice too much, he had my hands strapped again, but this time beside me and I'd take that over having them above my head any day.

"Better?" He asked.

I nodded. "But my shoulder—"

"Oh, yes, your shoulder," he smiled sardonically. "Bite this," he grabbed a blanket, shoving it at my mouth. I bit down on the fabric as he shoved my shoulder back into place. The blanket muffled my scream and Travis laughed. The bastard received some kind of sick twisted joy upon seeing people in pain.

He took the blanket and dropped it on the floor. "I'll be back soon." He bent, brushing his lips over my cheek. Bile rose in my throat, but I was careful to school my features. He had to believe I was giving in to him. It was my only hope of survival.

"Travis?" I said in a small meek voice, trying to play the damsel in distress.

"Yes," he stopped by the door, the tray in his hands.

"I'm really bored. Do you think I could have a TV or some books? Something?" I held my breath, hoping he didn't blow up at my request.

He smiled like the damn cat that at the canary. "If you keep up good behavior, I'm sure we can work something out."

With that, he left.

I let out a sigh of relief.

He hadn't said no, and he hadn't blown up, and for now I was able to move my arms more freely. I hoped I could keep up my acting. I stared at the window, covered by a heavy curtain, wondering whether it was day or night…wondering what Caeden was doing, and praying he'd find me in time.

SEVENTEEN.

I ran the sander over the wood again and again, the buzzing of the motor loud enough to momentarily block out my thoughts. I didn't feel human anymore. Sophie had been gone for two whole weeks, and I had nothing to show for my efforts of trying to find her. It was like she'd become a ghost. I'd checked out the shack he'd held her in before, nothing. I kept checking though—for any sign that someone had been there. I'd even went to Travis' parents' house—well, what *had* been their home before they died. That turned out to be a dead end too. As was the cave where he'd been with his mutants. Travis had a talent for evading me, and it was really pissing me off. Sophie was strong, and I prayed that she wasn't giving up on me—I'd never forgive myself if she did.

The whir of the sander cut off and I turned sharply to see Nolan standing by the outlet, the plug clasped in his hand.

"Oops," he smirked.

"What do you want?" I gave him the iciest glare I could.

"You've been holed up in here for two days. I thought I should check on you…" He paused. "What the hell is it that you're doing?"

I sighed, knowing he wouldn't go away if I ignored him. "I'm making a crib for the baby."

Nolan frowned and his brows formed a line as he contemplated what he was going to say next. Something told me I wasn't going to like it one bit.

"Do you think that's wise?" He finally said a few minutes later.

"What do you mean?" I asked, confused.

"Well," he swung the cord around, "you know…they might not come…*back*."

All the blood drained from my body, or at least it felt like that. "They're coming back."

"Caeden," he dropped the cord, and came closer to me, "you need to prepare yourself for—"

"No," I shook my head. "No. I don't need to prepare myself for anything."

He stopped, tilting his head to study me. "I just think—"

"I don't have time to listen to this." I put the sander down and strode around him. "Why don't you get out of my house and leave me alone? Huh? How does that sound?"

"Caeden, I'm your *friend*," he grabbed my shoulder, digging his fingers in so I couldn't move. "I'm going to sound like a chick saying this, but I'm really worried about you," he looked me up and down.

I knew what he saw, and smelled. My jeans and shirt were covered in stains, my hair was greasy and hung limply in my eyes because I hadn't gotten it cut in way too long, and I smelled like I hadn't showered in a week...which was exactly when I'd showered last.

"You don't need to worry about me. I'm fine." I roughly shook off his hold. I knew I was being an ass, but I couldn't help it. I didn't need Nolan, or anyone, worrying about me. That only managed to make me feel guilty—and I already felt guilty enough losing Sophie. I knew I wasn't the one that was with her when she was taken, but I should have been a damn tyrant and not let her leave. I'd worried about her getting too weak going out for too long, but I hadn't believed something like this could happen and that made me so naïve it was laugh worthy. Clearly, I truly wasn't cut out to be an Alpha.

"You're not fine." Nolan grabbed me again and this time, he wasn't nearly as gentle. He shoved me into the wall hard enough that the drywall caved a bit where my shoulder hit it. He held me up by the collar of my shirt and glared at me. "Why is it so hard for you to admit that you're not okay? It doesn't make you weak. You have a pack for a reason, Cay-berry, *use* them to get your girl back. Sulking like a baby isn't helping Sophie and it isn't helping you feel better. You need to do something!" He shoved me again, still holding onto my shirt. It was like he thought he could shake some sense into me.

"I'm trying to do something!" I yelled. "I've *been* trying to do something! There's only so much I can do before—" I stopped myself. I couldn't say it.

"Before what? Before you give up?"

I nodded. Looking back at the half built crib. "I *have* to believe they're alive, but it's getting harder to think I'm ever going to find them."

"God, you're such a Debby Downer," he shook me again. I knew I could shake him off in a second, but for some reason I didn't. I think somehow, I knew I needed to hear what he had to say even if it hurt to hear. "You're *sulking* and *pouting* while your wife, your *mate*, is out there fighting for her life against a sociopath. Think about that." He gave me one last hard shove before letting me go. Shaking his head as if he couldn't believe what an idiot I was, he left the garage.

I let out a deep pent up breath and stared up at the ceiling. I didn't know what more I could do, except tear the world apart to find her. And I'd do it, because I'd do anything for Sophie.

I felt a new resolve roll through my body.

I'd find her and she'd be fine. So, would Beau.

And I'd gladly watch the life drain from Travis' eyes when I got my hands on him.

* * *

"Where are you going?" Nolan stood at the bottom of the stairs with his arms crossed over his chest. He was starting to feel like an annoying babysitter.

"Why does it matter to you?" I strode right past him, heading for the garage.

"Because I'm your friend. If you're going somewhere, I'm going with you."

"I don't need you to come with me." The duffel bag of clothes thumped against my thigh. "I can handle this just fine on my own."

"Yeah, just like you've been handling everything just fine on your own. You need to stop going off by yourself." He shimmied around me so that he stood between the door and me. "If you don't want me to go with you, then ask Bentley, or your brother. *Someone.* You don't have to do this by yourself, Caeden. You have a pack for a *reason,* utilize them. A lone wolf is a dead wolf, you know that."

I swallowed thickly. "What do they say about lone tigers?"

"That they're super smart and kick ass," he smirked.

"Fine," I sighed dejectedly, "you can come, but if you piss me off I might punch you in the face just for the fun of it."

Nolan grinned. "I wouldn't expect anything else." Eyeing my bag, he said, "Looks like I better pack some clothes. Apparently you're not planning on coming back for a while."

I shrugged. "I thought I should be prepared."

"Don't. Leave." He enunciated each word carefully as he backed away from the door. He eyed me, daring me to leave without him. I'm not gonna lie, I thought about it. I didn't need to the extra baggage of Nolan breathing down my neck and criticizing every decision I made. But I figured he'd give me the third degree if I did, and I didn't need to hear it.

He returned not even two minutes later. "Ready."

"Don't make me regret this," I warned him, grabbing the key fob for my Jeep.

"Never, Cay-berry. Let's go on a road trip." He smiled giddily. "I hope you have some M&Ms."

Yeah, I was *so* going to end up punching him in the face.

* * *

"This is where they kept her the first time, isn't it?" Nolan asked, hanging back behind me.

"Yeah." I bent down, rubbing my fingers in the dirt. I'd been here a few times in the past two weeks. Each time I was hoping to find *something*, but I always turned up empty. She wasn't here. Travis wasn't here. And there was no sign that mutants had *ever* been here. This place was abandoned. If you entered the shack—it was too small to even be considered a cottage or house—there was still a stain on the floor where Travis' father had bled out. The body was gone though, either taken by his pack, or eaten by scavengers. A knife speared the door and the wood was tinted a dark rust color in places. I was sure it was a result of Travis killing his father. Maybe he'd pinned his head there—that sounded like something a sociopath like Travis would do.

I straightened, tilting my head back and breathing in the cold air. Over a year ago, he'd held her here and I'd nearly lost my girl before I even had the chance to tell her I loved her. I knew now why so many people said to make every moment count—you never knew which moment would be your last.

"What are you hoping to find here?" Nolan asked, his boots crunching the ground beneath their soles.

I turned my head to look over my shoulder at him. Squinting at the brightness of the sun, I replied, "Nothing. I know I'll find *nothing*. But being here, it gives me clarity." I swallowed thickly and went back to drawing random designs in the dirt. The ground was cold and unyielding, but I found something satisfactory in forcing it to move. I didn't know what I was drawing and I didn't care. It was a release.

"I don't follow." He crouched beside me, his breath forming fog in the cold air.

"Because, this is where I found her before. If I found her once, I can find her again...or so I keep telling myself."

"You will find her again." I saw him look at me out of the corner of my eye but I refused to meet his gaze.

"I know," I finally said.

But what we both left unspoken was would I find her alive?

I slowly stood, gazing around at the barren trees. I knew ahead of me was the makeshift grave where Leslee Grimm was buried. In the end, she'd turned out to be a good person and didn't deserve the demise she met—death by the hand of her own husband. I was convinced Peter and Travis Grimm were the most sadistic people to ever walk the planet. They didn't care who they hurt or who they killed. I wondered how many they'd killed that we'd never know about. And look at all the innocent lives lost with Travis' need to make mutants. I didn't understand how anyone thought killing someone was okay. I guess that made me a hypocrite, I'd killed before, but because I *had* to. Not because I wanted to, and there was a big difference.

I came to my feet and walked swiftly over to where I knew leaves and other debris hid the cellar door. I brushed them out of my way until I found the door and thrust it open. I descended into its damp depths, letting my eyes adjust to the darkness. If I inhaled I could just pick up the lingering scent of cookies—of Sophie. My throat constricted painfully and I knew I was about thirty seconds away from having a breakdown. I didn't need Nolan too see me lose it like this, so I carefully schooled my features as his feet thumped on the steps behind me.

"Whoa," he breathed, taking in the medieval looking gurney Sophie had been strapped to. "That's..."

"Creepy?" I supplied, sweeping my fingers along the metal.

"Yeah, definitely creepy. It reminds me of a horror movie, and knowing what happened to Sophie..." I saw him shrug out of the corner of my eye. "That's tough."

"You have no idea," I whispered.

Being here, seeing this, smelling her scent—it was getting to me. I felt sick to my stomach.

"Are you ready to head back?" Nolan asked.

"No," I shook my head, still looking around the small damp space. "I-I-need to be here for a little while longer."

Nolan leaned against one of the dirt walls, not saying a word. I think he knew I needed this. Although, anymore I didn't know what exactly it was I needed. True, like I told him, being here gave me hope that since I'd found her once I could find her again...but there was more to it than that. I just didn't know what the *more* was.

My eyes scanned over the metal table and my breath caught at the sight of several dark hairs clinging to the corner. There were still bloodstains on the table—blood my sweet Sophie had bled out. She hadn't deserved that and she certainly didn't deserve whatever shit it was that Travis was dealing her now.

I ran my finger along the cold slab, stopping when I reached the strands of hair. My throat clenched painfully and I couldn't breathe.

A strangled cry bubbled out of my throat, and my shoulders tensed together knowing Nolan was once again seeing me breakdown. I *couldn't* be strong no matter how hard I tried. Sophie was my mate, and without her I didn't know how to function. I knew that was a silly thing to think. I'd certainly functioned normally before I met her. But once she came into my life, she made me *better*. She made me a better brother, son, friend, and lover. She *owned* me, even though she didn't know it. Having her, and losing her, was the most painful thing I'd ever experienced. And knowing that she was somewhere *suffering* tore me apart.

I rubbed my chest; worrying about her and Beau was making my heart squeeze painfully. Could shifters have a heart attack? If we could, I was pretty sure I was about a second away from having one.

"You okay?" Nolan asked from the shadows.

What was the point in lying? "No. I'm not okay. In fact, I'm not sure I'm ever going to be okay again."

"You're going to find her." His voice was full of a determination I was lacking at the moment. I shouldn't have come here again, and certainly shouldn't have come into the cellar. This wasn't healthy for me. "You know that."

It was a statement, not a question, but I found myself answering anyway. "I know," because I'd never stop looking for my she-wolf, "but when I do find her, how much damage will have already been done to the both of us? And I'm not talking about the physical here. I know we can both handle that. But it's the scars inside—the ones no one can see—that tear into you and rip you apart, never healing."

"Sophie's a fighter," he clapped me on the shoulder, "she's feisty and that girl has a fire in her. If anyone can go through something traumatic and come out okay, I know it's Sophie. And you can too, Caeden. You're way stronger than you give yourself credit for. You're an amazing Alpha, nothing like the shitty one you believe you are. You expect too much of yourself. You're young, and this life isn't easy." He swallowed thickly. "You've been dealt a lot of shit, Caeden, and I understand why you're losing it right now. But Sophie needs you to keep your head on straight. Wherever she is, she's in no shape to fight or get away—it's your job to help her."

"I *know* that," I growled.

I was getting really sick and tired of these lengthy pep talks from Nolan. Had he spent a summer being a camp counselor or something? Where did he come up with this stuff?

"I know she needs me right now, but the problem is I don't know what to do. I don't even know *where* she is. And until I find out where Travis is keeping her, I can't very well come up with a plan."

Nolan sighed. "Just know, you have a pack standing beside you, and you have me too. That is if you want this tiger's help," he winked.

Leave it to Nolan to lecture me like he's my dad and then crack such a corny joke.

"Of course I want your help," I turned away from him, reaching out to stroke the strands of hair still clinging to the table. I was kind of amazed that they were still here. It had been over a year since Sophie was held here—but this place, it was like it was stuck in time. It would always serve as a disturbing memorial to what Sophie had suffered.

I closed my eyes, remembering everything Travis had done to her before. She still hated seeing the word *liar* carved into her arm. I knew though, that what she'd suffered then in no way compared to how she was suffering now. Travis thrived on causing pain and Sophie was incredibly weak right now. If we lost the baby because of Travis I could not be held accountable for my actions. I'd lose it. I already felt like I'd had so much ripped away from me—my dad, my youth, my mate—I couldn't bear the thought of losing my child as well. Especially before I even had the chance to get to know him.

My stomach clenched again and I thought for sure I was going to throw up this time, but I didn't.

It was scary to think that one person held the fate of the rest of your life in their hands. Travis had all the power right now. And me? I had nothing.

I grabbed the lingering strands of Sophie's hair and clasped them tightly in the palm of my hands.

"Let's go."

EIGHTEEN.
Sophie

The door to my cell—I refused to think of it as a guestroom—opened and Travis smiled brightly at me. I forced my own smile, trying to act like the meek docile creature that I was not.

"I brought you ice cream. It's vanilla." He sat down beside me, the bed dipping precariously to the right, but since I was still chained to the bed I didn't fall. Travis had removed the chains a few times to treat my bruised and chafed wrists—since I wasn't healing like a shifter normally would—but it kind of defeated the purpose because he always chained me right back up. There was a bathroom attached to the bedroom and he let me shower every other day. I relished those moments when I could get out of the bed and walk. My legs had grown weak and it was a struggle, but I enjoyed the burn.

I wasn't sure how long I'd been here…wherever here was…but if my calculations were correct, and based on the size of my ever increasing stomach, I'd say I'd been here a month. A whole freakin' month. With Travis.

He hadn't hit me much lately. Sometimes I said something smart, because I couldn't help myself, and he'd slap me. But I'd take it. This wasn't like the last time. I wasn't being tortured. In fact, it was like I was being cared for. Sometimes, I saw him greedily staring at my stomach and it scared me. Did Travis want Beau? And if so, what for? What scared me about that scenario was if I was here long enough to deliver Beau, would I then become disposable to Travis?

"Open up," Travis demanded, the spoon hovering in front of my lips. I half expected him to make choo choo noises, but that would just be silly...although, probably not any sillier than the fact that Travis was feeding me ice cream. Had I stepped into an alternate reality or something? I was starting to miss Crazy Travis—at least I understood that one. This one was a stranger.

I opened my mouth before he became angry and smacked me or flicked ice cream in my hair.

"Good?" He asked when I'd swallowed.

"Mhmm," I nodded.

He gave me another bite.

Once all the ice cream was gone, I asked, "Where-where am I?"

"Oh, come on Sophie, you know I can't tell you that," he patted my cheek like I was a small child—although, it was a little more than a pat since my cheek was left with a sting. "Good girls know better than to ask questions."

"Sorry," I bowed my head, my lashes fanning my cheeks as I tried to appear innocent. I needed to gain his sympathy, which was the dumbest thing ever since he had *kidnapped* me. Ugh.

"It's okay," he gently brushed my hair back from my forehead and took my chin between his warm fingers so I was forced to look at him. "I understand why you're curious. I would be too. But those questions will get you into trouble and you don't want that, do you?"

"No," I shook my head, trying to hide my revulsion at being touched by him.

"I'm glad you understand." He leaned closer to me and my body stiffened. I expected him to try to kiss me, but he didn't. He stopped, inhaling the air swirling around us. "You smell so good. So sweet." Yeah, and that's not creepy at all.

"Uh...thanks?" What the heck was supposed to say? I didn't want to piss him off and I'm pretty sure saying nothing would have made him mad.

"I'm sure you're thirsty. I'll be back with some water." He grabbed the bowl off the side table and left the room.

My stress didn't ease, knowing he'd be back soon.

He *had* brought me a TV in here, *but* he only turned it on when he felt like it and always put it on some random channel that ended up making me fall asleep out of boredom. Well, played Travis. Well, freakin,' played.

Until you were alone, with just your thoughts, you didn't realize what true boredom was. This was hell...or at least my version of it. And it wasn't like Travis really talked to me much when he visited, and I didn't say much to him either since I was scared of making him mad. There was a lot I was dying to ask him, but I knew if I did, he'd probably slit my throat. I was the most curious about the mutants. Where were they? Were they here, in this house, existing alongside me? Or did he keep them somewhere else? If they weren't here, then who *was* here? Because from the noises I heard, it was blatantly obvious that Travis wasn't the only person who existed outside this room. I wondered if I'd live long enough to get those questions answered. It was a morbid thought to have. But I'd been here so long, and with Travis' temper, I figured it was only a matter of time before he went nutso on me. He'd been relatively tame with me—even the slaps lately had hardly been worth complaining about. I wondered what that meant, and figured it couldn't possibly be anything good.

I glanced down at my prominent bump, biting my lip as I fought tears. Would I ever get to see my baby? Hold him? Kiss him? My throat constricted painfully. I was only staying sane by *not* thinking about those kinds of things. But the longer I was here, the harder it was to ignore such morbid thoughts.

The door opened again, and just like every other time, my heart skipped a beat in my chest. Each time the door opened, I expected it to be the last time.

Travis appeared with a glass full of ice water. I licked my lips as I watched a trickle of condensation snake its way down the clear glass and soak into the skin of Travis' hand. I was *so* thirsty. In fact, I was so dehydrated that if I wasn't chained to this bed and was capable of more strength than what it took to swat a fly, I would so tackle Travis to the ground and kill him for the water. Another thing I had learned, going without water was more painful than any of the physical stuff. My throat burned with my need for the simple substance.

"Here." Travis placed a pink bendy straw between my lips. Who would've thought that a sociopath would own brightly colored bendy straws? This guy was so difficult to figure out.

Once all the water was gone, I mewled in protest.

"More," I croaked hoarsely. I wanted to snatch the glass from his hands and crunch on the ice. "I need more," I begged. A single tear escaped my eye and his thumb flicked out to wipe it away. So quick I couldn't be sure I saw right, his thumb was in his mouth. Did he seriously just *lick* my tear off his finger? Um, gross.

"Sorry, no can do, the boss man wouldn't like that," he quipped.

Boss man?

"Boss man?" I voiced.

Travis paled, his dark eyes threatening to pop out of his skull. "Don't ask questions!" He yelled, spit flying everywhere. My cheek stung and then began to throb and I realized he'd slapped me. "Don't. Ask. Questions." He repeated, each word punctuated by a heavy breath. His face was quickly going from white, to pink, to a dangerous red color.

Finally, after staring at me for a minute, he turned sharply and left the room. The door slammed closed behind him.

I guessed all my good behavior had been for nothing.

I began to cry, pulling at the chains. I didn't care that it hurt my wrists. I needed to feel the pain to remind me that I was indeed still alive. A scream tore out of my throat. I think I was close to losing what was left of my sanity.

"Let me out!" I shouted, rattling the chains. "Let me out! Let me out! Let me *out!*"

I began to cry, unable to help myself. "Please," I begged no one, "let me out. I want to go *home*," my voice cracked.

I wanted Caeden. I wanted home. I wanted security.

Tears coursed down my cheeks, soaking the thin shirt I wore—a shirt that wasn't even my own. For some reason I wondered whose it was. It certainly wasn't Travis', it was too small for that. Did that mean there was a female here? One who might possess some empathy and help me out of here? Oh, who was I kidding? If there was a female here— wherever here was—she was just as crazy as Travis and in no way would help me.

My tears dried up and I began to hiccup. "Caeden, where are you?"

* * *

Caeden

I needed to kill something.

No, not something, someone.

Someone with blond hair and black eyes.

My fist flew into the bag again and Bentley grunted from the impact. "Dude, I think that hit my kidney," he said breathlessly.

"I. Don't. Care." I punched the bag over and over again, hoping I could punch the anger out of me. No such luck though. I'd been at it for a good two hours and I was still pissed and exhaustion had yet to set in.

Bentley grunted again and released the bag. It flew back at me and before I could move, it slammed into my chest, knocking me to the ground.

"What the hell?" I gasped; rubbing the sore spot on my chest that I could tell was already bruising.

147

"You need a reality check," Bentley stood above me, his arms crossed over his chest as he sent me an icy glare. "Punching the shit out of that thing," he pointed at the slightly swaying bag, "isn't going to make you feel better."

I clenched my teeth, my nostrils flaring with anger. He was right. "What do you expect me to do? I can't find her! I can't feel her! Even her familiar can't find her! She's *gone*," I croaked like a big old baby, "and there's nothing more I can do."

"There's always something you can do," Bentley whispered.

"Like what?" I sighed, running my fingers through my hair. "I've been everywhere I know to go and there's no sign of her or Travis. They're just gone. Poof! Non-existent!"

"Maybe you should talk to the elders," he started, and when I opened my mouth to cut him off, he gave me a look that said I'd regret it later. I knew when Bentley got like this that I shouldn't push him. "There might be something helpful in one of the legends. Maybe something that would help you locate her."

I shook my head, letting out a sigh. "I've read those things so many times, looking for information on the mutants that I practically have them memorized. There's nothing in there about locating person."

Bentley nodded. "Okay, then. At least stop moping. I know it sucks that you haven't found her yet—heck, Chris has been sick since she went missing because she's been so worried—but you have to stay optimistic."

"I'm an optimistic person by nature," I shook my head, slowly rising to my feet, "but even the most positive person loses hope after a while. And once you've lost hope—"

"You've lost everything," Bentley finished.
"Exactly," I nodded, cracking my knuckles.

Bentley appeared thoughtful for a moment. "Why don't you stay with Chris and I for a while? It's not good for you to be holed up in that house, making furniture all day. We have an extra bedroom. We wouldn't bother you."

"I don't know—"

"Don't make an excuse. I'm not saying you need to move in, but a few days might do you some good."

He was right. I really did need to get out of the house. The only time I left was to come here, to the gym, and to look for Sophie, which always left me feeling exhausted and defeated since everything led to a dead end. I didn't understand how they were just…gone. For all I knew, they were states away, or even a whole other country. Looking for Sophie had become hopeless. Until she had the baby, or…or Travis killed her, I wouldn't know anything. I was stuck in limbo, waiting for *something*. I didn't like this one bit, but there was nothing more I could do and I had to face reality. This time, Sophie probably wasn't coming home and neither would our son.

* * *

Bentley drove me home to get some clothes and the dogs. I think he was afraid I'd change my mind and not come. Driving me assured that I couldn't get away and make an excuse. He thought he was sneaky and didn't know what he was up to, but I wasn't dumb.

As we drove to Bentley and Christian's place, I frowned at the melting snow. It signified that spring was fast approaching. So much time had passed since Travis first took Sophie and it made me sick to my stomach to imagine what my she-wolf was going through. Was she chained to a table like she had been before? Locked in a room alone? Beaten? Sore?

"Remember when we were kids and all we could talk about was when we would first shift?" Bentley asked, momentarily distracting me from my thoughts.

"Yeah," I nodded, watching the trees whip past us.

"I miss those days," he mused. "We were so innocent to the responsibility that comes with shifting."

"Tell me about it," I muttered. I'd been so excited for my first shift. Never in a million years did I think that two years later I'd be taking over my dad's position as Alpha. I hadn't been ready for *that* responsibility, and even now I still felt inadequate for the position. I wondered if there had ever been as shitty of an Alpha as me.

"I think we need to get that back."

"Get what back?" I shook my head, forcing myself to focus on his words. "The...freedom...the innocence...the *desire* to be what we are. Let's go for a run," his voice had become excited

"Where? I thought you lived in a neighborhood? We can't exactly run through the streets as wolves, we'd get shot, and while that might not be fatal for us it would be awfully inconvenient."

Bentley shook his head. "We do live in a neighborhood, but there are woods all around us." He let go of the wheel to encompass the mountainous area surrounding us.

"I don't—"

He was already pulling off the road, and since I didn't feel like arguing, I let him.

He put his truck in park and unbuckled his seatbelt. Looking at me, he said, "Fun. We're going to have *fun*. Extra emphasis on the *fun*, in case you missed it."

"I got it," I shook my head, following him out of the truck.

I followed him into the woods, staring up at the glowing orange of the setting sun. It was beautiful, reflecting the promise of hope—of a new day. I wish I could still feel hope, but I'd stopped a while ago. I knew that was wrong of me, but I couldn't help it. If I could *feel* Soph, then I might think differently, but right now I was convinced that she was lost to me forever.

"What are you doing?" Bentley asked as he turned around to see me staring at the sunset.

"Nothing," I shook my head, forcing my feet forward. I stripped off my clothes and folded them into a neat pile, while Bentley did the same. A shiver ran down my spine as I began to shift. I'd always loved shifting—but lately, everything had made me hate what we are. I fell to the ground on four paws, blinking my eyes as everything came into focus. Seeing, as a wolf, was so different than seeing as a human. Colors were more muted, but somehow sharper. The outlines of the leaves on trees caught my eye, their jagged edges something you couldn't see with human eyes.

Come on, Caeden! Bentley called, running ahead of me, his black form a blur. *Let's race!*

I didn't feel like racing, but the challenge in the tone of his voice was something I couldn't resist. My feet soared forward, like they had a mind of their own, carrying me away from all my problems.

Bentley was right. This was freedom and I'd forgotten that. My dad wouldn't want that for me. He'd want me to embrace what I was. The good, the bad, and the ugly. There were good and bad things about *anything* you did or were, but being able to shift…there was something magical about that. Everyone believed we were a fairytale. But shifters were real. We were anyone and everyone. And even humans had a little shifter inside them, because we all could identify as something else.

The ground thumped beneath my feet and my tongue lolled out of my mouth. The wind raised my fur and my eyes closed momentarily—relishing in the feel of it.

Do you feel it yet? Bentley's voice sounded in my head as I approached his dark form.

Yeah. Yeah, I do.

I let everything else disappear, savoring the freedom of the moment. Nothing else mattered in this moment. I just ran, playing like a little kid. I needed this after everything I'd been going through.

It sucked that there was so much out of my control. I was a leader, and it was in my blood to stand up and fight. Sitting back and doing nothing was not sitting well with me.

I jumped over a fallen tree, letting my body fly through the air for a moment. I wished I could pause time and just linger here for a moment, floating through the air. But wishes never come true. My feet touched the ground once more and I surged forward. I'd lost sight of Bentley and I wasn't sure if he was still in front of me or behind me. I didn't care though. I wasn't racing. I was *feeling*.

I didn't know how long we were out there, but by the time we headed back to where we'd stashed our clothes, I was exhausted…in a good way. My muscles burned, but I enjoyed the small twinge of pain.

We climbed back into his truck and headed to the apartment. Because I'd been so worried about Sophie, I hadn't seen their apartment…in fact, I don't think I'd ever even congratulated them on getting married. I was a horrible friend. But I knew Bentley understood.

I hopped out of the truck and slung my bag over my shoulder. I reached out, stopping Bentley. His questioning gaze met mine.

I swallowed thickly, the apology thick on my tongue. "I-I-want to apologize for being so out of it. Thanks for being there for me and I'm really happy for you and Christian." A lump formed in my throat. Christian had been with Sophie when Travis took her. And while I knew it was wrong to blame her, a part of me couldn't help it.

Bentley looked at me for a moment and finally nodded. "You've had a lot going on, Caeden. I know that. And I know it's…" He paused. "I know it has to be hard for you to be happy for me right now."

"It shouldn't be hard though," I whispered, glancing down at the ground, ashamed of myself. "You're my best friend, and despite all the crap going on in my life right now, I should be able to be happy for you."

"Stop," he said sternly, sounding more like a father than a friend. "If the situation was reversed, I know how I'd feel. I understand that right now, you're more lost in your thoughts than present in the real world. I *get* it. Okay?"

I nodded. "Now come on," he slung an arm across my shoulders, pulling me forward, "my hot wife made chili for dinner and I'm *starving*."

With a chuckle, I let him lead me up the stairs to the second floor apartment. There wasn't anything special about it. The walls were standard beige and the furniture was all hand-me-down. In that moment, I silently promised to find them a better place to live with nicer stuff...as soon as Sophie was back in my arms. Until I held my she-wolf again, I wasn't sure I'd be capable of doing anything.

"Hi, Christian," I said softly.

The pretty blonde girl smiled at me. She'd been awkward around me ever since Travis took Sophie. I knew she believed that I blamed her—and while a part of me did, it was a very small part. I knew how cunning Travis could be, and the poor girl probably never saw it coming.

"Hi." Her voice was barely above a whisper.

The three of us stood in an awkward triangle, waiting for someone else to do something first.

Finally, I let out a breath and asked, "So, where's the chili?"

Christian smiled softly and nodded at the small stovetop. "It's ready. Bowls are in that cabinet," she pointed. "Spoons are there, and the cornbread should be ready in a few minutes."

"Good," I nodded, "because I'm starving."

She laughed—and the sound of it was slightly forced. "I hope I made enough then. I have a hard enough time keeping this one fed," she went into Bentley's arms.

I closed my eyes, my gut clenching. I wanted to hold Sophie like that. I wanted to feel her body pressed against mine. I wanted to soak in her warmth and inhale her delicious smell of cookies. Being without her was slowly eating me alive. This time was worst than the last—not because she'd been gone longer, but because this time we were *bound* and not having her close felt like something was tugging me in all directions…trying to reach out and find her. But I couldn't truly feel her, not as long as Beau resided safely inside her.

I slowly opened my eyes, swallowing thickly. I would not break down. I'd been doing too much of that. I needed to keep my head on straight—because if I did, then maybe I'd be able to find Soph, despite Beau interfering with our connection. I had to find her. *Them.* I had to find *them.*

I stepped forward, grabbed a bowl, and filled it with chili. I went about my business like I wasn't freaking out on the inside. Bentley and Christian watched me carefully, like they were waiting for me to snap and throw the bowl of hot chili on them. I hated that my best friend and his wife felt that way. I wasn't an angry person by nature, but these past weeks—*months*—had taken a major toll on my mental state. I was beginning to lose sight of the man I'd been, and an angry bitter version was taking his place.

Instead of looking forward to the birth of my son, I was wondering if I'd ever even get to see him. It was painful to think I might lose my son before I even had the chance to meet him and that his mother might be lost with him. What would I do without them? Who would I be? A wolf without his mate isn't a good thing. I think I'd slowly go crazy without them.

I bit my lip sharply, drawing blood, and looked down at the barely touched bowl of homemade chili. So much for the appetite I'd worked up.

Bentley and Christian sat down across from me, watching me with sharp eyes.

I forced myself to bring the spoon to my mouth and eat the chili. I avoided their wondering gazes, not in the mood to talk. My reprieve from feeling was gone. I wasn't a wolf anymore. I was back in my human shell, trapped here where I could do nothing but wait. And waiting really sucked.

NINETEEN.
Sophie

Travis sat on the end of the bed, staring out the window. This was the first time he'd ever opened the curtains and the sun nearly blinded my eyes. I had grown so weak that I couldn't even lift my hand to shield my eyes. Not that I'd be able to anyway, being chained up and all.

He'd been sitting there for at least ten minutes. He didn't say anything. He just sat there, staring into space, lost in his thoughts.

"Sophie?" The sound of my name startled me and I jumped slightly.

"Yes?" I croaked.

"I want to show you something." He still didn't turn to look at me, his gaze was fixed firmly on the window. "Come outside?"

"I-I don't think I can move," I admitted, even though the thought of getting outside sounded heavenly. I hadn't felt the sun on my face or breathed in fresh air in months.

He turned to look at me for the first time since he'd opened the curtains.

"I can carry you."

He was already standing, undoing my bindings, and holding out his arms to gather me against his chest. I cringed, unable to control my reaction. I didn't want to be that close to Travis.

He pulled me into his arms and my head lolled against his muscular chest. His arms were strong and firm around me. If it weren't for the fact that he didn't smell like Caeden, if I closed my eyes I could pretend he was.

I tried to look around as he carried me from the room, but I was too weak to move my head.

My head thumped against his chest and I knew we had to be going down steps. There was a creak and then I felt fresh air touch my cheeks. I inhaled the air greedily, letting it flood my lungs. It felt so good to be outside—to feel the air and to hear the sounds of nature. If only I was strong enough to pull out of his arms and run away from this nightmare.

He carried me further and further away from the house and into the woods. He was surprisingly tender and made sure not to jostle me. The moments like this made me wonder if Travis really was the bad guy. Maybe he was just completely misunderstood and there was more to him than we knew. I guessed I wanted to believe there was good in everyone.

"We're here," he whispered in my ear, skimming his lips along my cheek. Ew.

He lowered me to the ground, but held tightly to my waist so that I didn't teeter back and forth.

I looked around at the mounds of dirt everywhere and felt completely confused. "I'm confused."

"I need you to understand why we're doing this, Sophie. I'm not evil—not completely at least," he shrugged, like it was something he said often and I shouldn't be completely freaked out.

"What is it that you're doing?" I asked, my heart racing rapidly in my chest.

"I wasn't making the mutants to kill you and Caeden, although I'd be lying if I said I wouldn't like to see him dead," he said quietly. "I got *permission* to make them."

"Permission? From who?" I continued to stare at the uneven mounds of dirt.

"From the elders," he whispered.

"Oh, God." I was going to throw up. "*Why?*"

"Because," his voice was steady and calm, "it's about time shifters were revealed to the world—that we're on top."

"I don't understand what you're saying." That was a lie. I knew what he was saying. But I needed to hear it.

"We're going to start a war with the humans, Sophie. We can't just walk out and transform, they'd hunt us down and kill us—or try to at least—but if we start a war, they'll have no choice but to bow down to our superiority. You and me, we could rule this world." His fingers skimmed over my collarbone and I shivered at the touch—and not the good kind of shivers that Caeden could produce from me. Anytime he touched me, it made me feel *dirty*. I didn't like it at all.

"You can't just start a war, Travis—"

"We *can* and we *will*," he growled.

"Where do the mutants come into this?" I asked, not wanting to make him angry.

"Well, when the humans see what we can transform them into—if they survive, that is—they'll obey us without hesitation. The ones that don't survive the transformation will end up here," he waved his hand at the mounds, "and honestly, this is probably better than turning into a mutant."

I pulled away from his hold and dropped to the ground, emptying the meager contents of my stomach. How could he be so calm about this? He was talking about murdering people and taking away their free will if they didn't comply with his wishes. Not just his wishes, but the wishes of the elders too. Oh, God, was Gram in on this too?

I didn't know I had anything else left in my stomach, but it came spewing up.

Travis bent down, rubbing my back in soothing circles. I stiffened at the touch, but I knew better than to shake him off.

"One day, you'll understand why I'm doing this."

"I will *never* understand—"

The color drained from my face as I felt a gush between my legs. "No," I whispered. "No, no, no, no. This *can't* be happening!" I looked down to see liquid stained slightly pink with blood. I wasn't sure that was normal.

But I didn't have time to ponder that, because my water had broke, and the baby was coming.

I looked up into Travis' eyes and he looked as shocked as I did.

Then, he smiled slowly. "Our son is coming."

I almost threw up again right then. "He is *not* your son," I spat.

"He will be."

That sounded entirely too ominous to me. Travis picked me up once more, carrying me away from the mounds of dirt that hid the dead humans. So many lives had already been lost, and I knew it was only going to get worse if we didn't end this.

I ended up back in the bed only he didn't chain me up this time.

It was suddenly hitting me that I had gone into labor. Beau was coming, and the only person I had to help me was Travis. Holy crap. I'd thought things were bad before, but this took it to a whole new level.

I knew in that moment that Travis was going to deliver my baby. Early, I might add. I knew there had to be at least a month before Beau was due, and Travis couldn't have any medical experience. What if something was seriously wrong with the baby? Oh. My. God.

I couldn't worry about the dead humans, mutants, elders, or the war that they wanted to rage against humans. Right now, all I could think about was the fact that Beau was in danger.

I took deep breaths—not to control the pain I was in, but in the hopes of dissipating some of the panic rolling through my body.

I couldn't believe I was having my baby here with no hospital in case anything went wrong. I didn't have Caeden by my side. I was alone, and scared to death that something might happen to my son.

The door to the room opened back up and Travis wheeled a metal cart into the room with all kinds of disturbing looking medical instruments. My heart skipped a beat. He'd been prepared for this.

I lay back, wishing I had the energy to crawl away from him.

"Everything will be just fine, Sophie," he assured me, pulling on scrubs.

I couldn't believe this was happening. Even though I knew exactly what was going on, it didn't seem real. I wanted to *believe* it wasn't real.

My abdomen clenched and I doubled over. This was awful, unlike anything I'd ever experienced. Tears coursed down my face.

"Shh, Sophie, it will be okay," Travis smoothed my hair out of my face.

"No, it won't," I sobbed, closing my eyes.

He continued going about, preparing the room to bring my son into the world. I just hoped Beau was okay. Although at this point, death might be a better option for him since he wouldn't be subjected to whatever Travis and the elders had planned. What an awful thing, to wish death for your child, but wouldn't you if you knew they'd be better off? I didn't even want to consider the different possibilities of why they'd want Beau.

I closed my eyes as another contraction hit me and a scream tore out of my throat. I didn't know much about pregnancy or babies, but I knew enough to know that things were moving way too fast.

Travis ripped my sweatpants off and I couldn't even grumble about being exposed to him. That wasn't important right now. Right now, all I could focus on was bringing Beau into the world—alive. I needed to hear him cry. I needed to see him and hold him. Breathe in his scent.

"Sophie, there's no time to give you any drugs." Travis explained in a gentle tone, smoothing my sweat drenched hair off my forehead. I didn't understand Travis at all. One moment he could be yelling and on the verge of losing it—the next he was actually...sweet. "The baby is coming now."

I nodded my head. I knew the baby was coming and there was nothing I could do to stop it.

I'd always been told that it took a while to deliver your first child, but no more than ten minutes could have passed since my water broke. I wondered if this was a shifter thing, or there was something *really, really* wrong. Despite the fact that death might be a better option for my child, I didn't want to lose him. It was selfish of me, but he was my *baby*.

Travis stuck an IV in my arm and I jumped, not expecting it.

He already had gloves on, one of those funny looking hats, and a mask covering his nose and mouth. He'd really thought of everything. I glanced at the corner of the room and saw one of those clear beds they put babies in when they're born as well as blankets and other things I couldn't see very well.

I was breathing deeply, trying to block out the pain and everything going on around me.

Right now I didn't need distractions. I needed to focus my strength on delivering Beau.

Travis adjusted my legs and muttered something I didn't hear. My vision was going spotty and I couldn't concentrate. The world around me was going in slow motion.

Oh no. The IV! He was drugging me! He had to be!

Travis' face appeared in front of mine. He said something else but it sounded like he was speaking to me from the end of a tunnel.

"Whhhaaat?" I tried to speak, but I wasn't sure the word actually left my mouth. My lips were numb. Why the hell were my lips numb? I thought he said there was no time for pain medicine? He had to have drugged me for an entirely different reason.

Everything felt out of my control. I was here, but I wasn't here. My vision was blurry and I couldn't focus on anything. Time was slowed down, but at the same time it was like it was sped up. Nothing made sense.

I felt pressure and a clenching in my gut. I wanted to cry from the strange feeling, but my body showed no reaction. My brain was active, but my body wasn't. It was like I was paralyzed.

I felt so out of control...like I was spinning through the air with no idea which way was up or down.

My breath stopped when a cry filled the room.

Beau.

My son, he was here, and he was crying. He needed me, his *mother*. I was a mom. Gosh, that was a strange concept. I really had a baby.

I tried to lift my arms, but they didn't move. I was broken, useless.

"B-b-beau." I tried to say his name, but the word left my lips sounding nothing like Beau. *Give me my son! I want my baby!* I screamed the words in my head, but they did no good. Travis couldn't hear me, and even if he could, he didn't care.

The cries grew quieter, disappearing farther away.

"W-wait," I muttered weakly. *Please, wait.*

My eyes closed and everything else ceased to exist.

TWENTY

I sat up straight, an awareness rocking me to my core—so much so that I fell out of the chair I was sitting in.

"Caeden?" Nolan questioned hesitantly, looking at me like I was crazy.

I put a hand to my chest, my cheeks stretching into a smile. "I feel her."

"Uh…"

"I *feel* her, Nolan!" I jumped up, excitement and adrenaline coursing through my veins. "This means I can find her!"

"Are you serious?!" He jumped up as well.

"I'm positive." I was grinning like a fool, but all of a sudden I frowned, because if I felt her then that meant… "No," I shook my head, dropping to my knees. "Beau."

"Oh, shit." Nolan muttered.

"We have to hurry," I exclaimed. I managed to get myself to my feet and I looked around frantically, wondering if I needed to take anything. I decided there wasn't time. "Come on, we have to go."

I ran out the back door of the house, transforming in mid air. Pieces of my clothes exploded, decorating the yard in a strange looking confetti. I vaulted over the fence, running through the woods so fast you would've thought the hounds of hell were chasing me. I forced myself to come to a stop so I could howl and call my pack. I didn't know what I was heading into and I needed everybody.

My legs were burning because I was running so fast. If someone had been hiding in the trees, watching me run by, all they would've seen was a gray blur.

What's going on? Bentley voiced. I could tell he was near his home and was racing to meet up with me.

I feel Sophie. I answered simply. *She's fading in and out, but I know she's close. We have to get there soon.*

He understood what I couldn't say. Sophie 'fading' was a bad thing. It meant she was barely hanging on and I had to hope and pray we reached her in time.

I didn't want to admit to myself that I was coming very close to losing her—and I might have already lost my son. It was unfair that one person—Travis—could destroy my whole world. If he was there—wherever there was—when I reached Sophie, I'd rip him into pieces and not even blink an eye. I had suffered too much because of him and I'd long ago reached my breaking point.

I didn't know you could run so fast. Nolan's voice filled my head.

There's a lot you don't know about me. Like the murderous thoughts I was currently thinking of. I wanted to see Travis' blood on my hands. I wanted to watch the light leave his eyes. I wanted to—

I came to a stop.

Holy shit.

What? Nolan and Bentley asked simultaneously. Several more voices echoed in my head but I couldn't focus on them.

I know where we're going.

Where? Bentley questioned, his voice laced with confusion.

The elders' headquarters. The elders occupied a small two-story house in the woods to conduct their business. It had been vacant for years, and no one else knew its location. They didn't live there full-time, but they spent most of their time there, which meant they were in on it just like I had suspected. I had been right all along about them and I should have trusted my gut. I'd never make that mistake again.

My anger spurned me on the last few miles. I came to a stop outside the house and transformed back into my human skin. I couldn't get inside the house quick enough. The place was deserted, but I knew Sophie was here.

I jogged up the steps and came to a stop outside a closed door with a deadbolt on it. It was unlocked, my stomach clenched. She'd been locked in here like some kind of animal. Someone had to be really sick to do that to another human being. I took a deep breath and opened the door, bracing myself for what I might encounter.

The room was empty, except for the lone form spread out on the bed. Blood was everywhere. Covering her legs, the sheets of the bed, and even the floor. Her skin was pale and her chest shuddered with shaky breaths. A noise I couldn't even begin to describe bubbled out of my throat. I ran to her side, taking her face between my hands. She was so tiny and fragile looking. She hadn't looked this breakable when I found her before. This was bad.

"Sophie, baby, can you hear me?" I lightly smacked her cheeks, trying to generate a response.

Bleary brown eyes peeked at me. They were fading, taking on the chalky tone of death.

"Sophie, stay with me," I pleaded, on the verge of tears. "I need you, baby. You have to stay with me. You can't leave me. I love you." Words tumbled out of my mouth without any control on my part. I needed her to hear my words and to grasp onto them so they could give her the strength she needed to live. She was my *life* and I couldn't live without her.

"B-b-b—"

She tried to speak, but couldn't form words. Her lips had taken on an unnatural blue tone, like someone who was too cold. I looked at the IV in her arm, it's liquid a strange pearly gray color. I ripped it out of her arm, tearing the plastic in the process, and some of the liquid sprayed on my hand. I screamed out in pain and glanced down at my hand to find it burned and blistered looking in the spots where the liquid had splashed it. My eyes widened. The liquid was laced with silver.

I knew Bentley was in the room behind me, I didn't know where the others were and frankly I didn't care.

"Bentley, I need you to stay with Sophie. I'll be right back. Just talk to her. Keep her eyes open. *Please*, don't let her leave me."

He nodded, taking in the seriousness of the situation. "Hurry."

I jogged back down the steps and into the room the elders used for meetings. There was a loose floorboard beneath the table and I had to crawl on my hands and knees to reach it. I yanked it up, tossing it to the side of me.

Vials of fairy dust met my eyes. It was gold in color and to a human they would have thought the tiny bottles were filled with sparkling glitter. But I knew better.

I grabbed all the vials, knowing I didn't need all of them, but there was no way I was leaving them here.

"Hurry, dude," Bentley warned when I topped the stairs.

My heart was racing so hard in my chest that I was scared it might give out and my blood roared in my eardrums. I dropped the vials on the bed and grabbed one, pulling out the cork. I sprinkled some of the gold dust over the small dot of a wound where the IV had been, before proceeding to pour the rest down her throat.

Within a minute color was returning to her cheeks and her breathing was evening out. I wasn't going to lose her. I wasn't. I wasn't. I wasn't.

Her eyes opened completely and the warmth of the brown made my heart skip a beat. They weren't dull like they had been.

"Caeden?" She croaked, her voice dry and shaky.

I couldn't say anything in response. I reached out, enveloping her in my arms. A sob escaped me and I didn't care if it wasn't very Alpha like to cry. I thought I'd lost my girl forever, but she was here in my arms, and she'd be fine.

"Where's Beau?" Her voice was quiet and hesitant, like she feared the answer.

I pulled back, taking her face between my hands. I didn't know what to say, because I didn't *know* anything about Beau. It was obvious he wasn't here and neither was Travis or any elders.

She took my silence as an answer and tears began to leak out of her eyes. I swiped them away, hating seeing her in so much pain. She buried herself into my arms and sobbed. Her tears soaked my bare skin and I brushed my fingers through her matted hair. "We're going to find him," I assured her. "I promise."

"Don't promise me that," she said weakly. The fairy dust had brought her back from the brink of death, but having silver sent directly into her veins was going to take some recovery time. "Don't promise me something you might not be able to keep."

I closed my eyes, her words like a punch to my gut. She was right though. Beau was with Travis, and chances were we'd never meet our son, because whatever Travis had planned couldn't be good.

"I'm so sorry, baby," I whispered, pressing kisses to the top of her head. She had no idea just how sorry I was for *everything*. Sophie might have always been going to be a shifter, but meeting me brought a lot of bad into her life. None of this would've happened if she'd never met me. I didn't deserve her love, because all I did was destroy her life. That didn't mean I was walking away though. I'd fight for this girl, for our love and for our lives, till my dying breath. Because that's what you did when you loved someone unconditionally. You didn't walk away because of the bad, you stood up and you fought.

I held her for as long as I could, breathing in her scent, but eventually, I knew we were going to have to leave.

"Can you shift?" I asked her, forcing her to meet my gaze.

She sniffled and shook her head. "I'm sorry, but I don't think I can. I'm too tired."

I grimaced. If she could shift it would speed up the healing process, but after everything she'd been through I wasn't going to push her.

I turned to Bentley, who had yet to leave my side. I didn't know what I'd do without that guy. He was more than my best friend—he was like a brother to me. "We're not too far from my mom's house. Go back there and get clothes for us," I pointed to me and Sophie, "and pick us up in Bryce's Jeep. It should be able to make it out here."

The house was located deep in the woods and the terrain was rough, making it nearly impossible to reach by car, but we had no choice.

He nodded and disappeared. I knew he'd hurry, but waiting was going to suck. All I wanted to do was get Sophie home and take care of her.

"Bryce!" I called for my brother. I needed his help and there was no way I was leaving Sophie here by herself. Now that I had her, I wasn't leaving her side. She was going to get so sick of me, but I didn't care.

"You called," Bryce's voice sounded at the bottom of the steps. "What do you need?"

"Travis isn't here, neither is...neither is Beau." Saying that made me want to throw up, but I had to be strong for Sophie. "I need you and the others to see if you can track him. Leave some behind to look around here for anything mysterious, like a tunnel or something. I wouldn't put anything past Travis."

"You got it, captain!" Bryce yelled up the steps and then the door slammed closed behind him.

"I'm so sorry," Sophie whispered. I turned to look at her and found her lower lip to be trembling. Tears glimmered in her eyes.

"Sorry?" I brushed her hair off her forehead with my fingers. "Baby, what do you have to be sorry about?"

"I couldn't fight back," she croaked. "He-he did something to Chris. Is she okay?" Color heated her cheeks as she began to panic.

"Shh," I hushed her. "Christian is fine. In fact, I'm surprised she hasn't busted in here to check on you. She's felt so guilty about what happened."

"Guilty?" Her brows furrowed in confusion. "But he *hurt* her. She couldn't do anything."

"No, she couldn't, and neither could you. Don't waste time worrying about things that were out of your control. Nothing was anybody's fault but Travis'."

She gasped, her eyes widening. "Caeden, he said—"

I put a finger to her lips, hushing her. I was desperate to know what she wanted to say, but I knew she needed to stay calm right now. "It's not important at the moment, she-wolf. You can tell me later."

"But—"

"No," I shook my head. "You need to focus on healing. Whatever you know, you're still going to know it when you feel better."

She nodded, lying on her side with her hands curled beneath her head. She looked so small and fragile—two things that didn't normally come to my mind when you thought of Sophie.

"We're never going to see him, are we?" She cried softly.

I swallowed thickly. "Don't think like that, Sophie."

"I didn't even get to hold him…or see him. I don't even know what he looks like." She began to sob and the sounds of her cries broke my heart. I hated seeing Sophie like this, and knowing there was nothing I could do to make her feel better. Nothing I said could make this better. I had never felt so…useless in all my life. We were mates, and we were always able to handle things together, but right now I had never felt so far removed from her. How do you comfort your wife over the loss of your child—a loss you're not even sure you need to grieve?

I took a deep breath, thinking through what I was about to say. "We're going to see him, Soph. He's out there and we're going to find him. You have nothing to worry about."

God, what a lie. We had everything to worry about.

I smoothed my finger over her cheek and she let out a small sigh as her eyes closed. I knew she had to be exhausted after everything she went through. She'd been with Travis for nearly three months and if it had felt like an eternity to me, it was ten times worse than that for her.

"Go to sleep, baby," I whispered in her ear. "I'll be right here. I'm not going anywhere."

"I don't want to sleep," she croaked, trying to crack her eyes open. "When I close my eyes all I see is…is him."

My breath came out shaky. She'd been traumatized by what happened to Logan, but this was something I wasn't sure time would ever heal. She might always be a little bit broken. But I'd love those broken pieces with every fiber of my being, and hopefully my love would heal her—maybe not the whole way, but enough that she'd be okay.

"I love you so much," I brushed my lips over hers.

Her eyes opened and her lashes fanned her cheeks as she blinked. "I know."

"And don't you ever forget it," I added.

"That would be impossible…" Her eyes closed once more and her breathing evened out so I knew she'd been unable to resist the lure of sleep.

I reached out and took her hand in mine. She was so bony and thin—but she'd gotten like that before Travis took her. I sent up a silent prayer that I'd felt her, and gotten here in time. I'd really almost lost her and I couldn't imagine my life without Sophie in it. It sure would be a lonely existence.

But now, we didn't have our son, and that left behind a feeling in the pit of my stomach that I couldn't begin to describe. I'd do everything I could to find him—just like I had with Sophie. But I had to be smarter about it this time. I couldn't go off the deep-end and not listen to anyone. I might be Alpha but we're a *pack*, which means we're supposed to work together, and I needed them to find Beau...and Travis, so I could destroy him once and for all.

This ended now.

And the elders were going down with him. I wasn't playing games anymore. I was standing up and fighting for what was *right*.

"Here."

I startled at the voice. I'd been so lost in my thoughts that I hadn't realized Bentley had returned. Some shifter I was.

He tossed the clothes at me and I quickly pulled on the jeans and shirt. I glanced down at Sophie's sleeping form. I hated to disturb her, but I didn't want to be here a second longer.

I shook her gently and her eyes opened slowly, blinking at me blearily.

"Whaaa?"

"Come on, baby, I need to get you dressed so we can get out of here."

"Oh," she shook her head.

"We'll be out in a minute." I told Bentley.

"I'll be outside if you need me."

I helped Sophie into a sitting position and removed the nasty blood and sweat soaked clothes from her body. She weakly raised her arms above her head and I pulled the sweatshirt over her, shielding her body. Bentley had also grabbed a pair of sweatpants that I was sure had belonged to my mom. They were too small to be mine. Thank God he'd been smart enough to pick something warm. I hadn't thought to tell him. Sophie held onto my shoulders as I helped her step into the pants.

I didn't bother to ask her if she could walk. I grabbed her up in my arms and cradled her against my chest. I hadn't even made it to the car before she was asleep again. Bentley helped me get her into the back of the Jeep so that I didn't hurt her.

Garrett, Sophie's dad, appeared behind some bushes. "Caeden, you're going to want to take a look at this."

I glanced at Sophie and back at Garrett. I didn't want to leave her, but I couldn't abandon my duties as Alpha either. I was torn on what to do.

Bentley grabbed my arm and forced me to look at him. "Go," he nodded towards Garrett. "I'll stay with her. You have nothing to worry about."

I let out a sigh of relief. I trusted Bentley.

"I'll be right back." I told him, but really the words were for my benefit.

I followed Garrett a ways into the woods before things opened up and several other shifters stood around, digging up mounds.

I was going to be sick. The smell—God, it was awful. The smell of decaying human flesh was something you could never forget.

I held my breath, shaking my head.

"How many?" I voiced.

"Too many," Garrett whispered.

"What do we do with them?" I asked. "Notify the police?"

"That seems like the best bet. These families…they deserve closure." Garrett stood back behind me, letting me take in the carnage around us. I refused to let myself count the mounds. I didn't want to know how many dead ones there were—or think about how many successfully turned mutants Travis might possess now.

I turned away from everything and started passed Garrett. "Take care of this. I trust your judgment, Garrett. Right now, I need to be with Sophie."

"We'll be by later," he assured me. "Tell her that her mom and I love her."

"I will," I shoved my hands in my jeans pockets.

I jogged back to the Jeep so that I could get there sooner. Bryce had returned with other wolves and I saw Bentley and Christian in the back of the Jeep with a sleeping Sophie.

"Hey," I said, coming to a stop in front of Bryce. "Find anything?"

He frowned, glancing down at the ground. I knew that didn't mean anything good. "We followed the trail for a mile or so and then it…it just…stopped."

"Stopped? What do you mean?" I fired questions at him.

"I mean, it *stopped*," he rolled his eyes at me. "The scent disappeared."

"How is that possible?" My body was tensing all over. How could someone disappear without a trace? No scent, no nothing?

Bryce shrugged. "I don't know. It's Travis. Why should we be surprised?"

I nodded. That was true. I scrubbed my hand over my face. "Look again."

"Again?" He raised a brow. "I don't think we're going to find anything new."

"I don't care. Do it," I raised my voice, knowing I needed to take on a demanding tone with Bryce.

"Whatever," he huffed, turning away from me and shifting. The other wolves followed after him.

I rubbed my face, closing my eyes, and let out a pent up breath. I felt like this whole thing had aged me twenty years. I got in the car and looked behind me at Bentley and Christian. "How is she? Has she woken up any?" I questioned.

"Sleeping like a baby," Bentley smiled. "I'm pretty sure she drooled on me."

Despite the dreariness of the situation, I managed to crack a small smile. "She *does* drool."

Before I drove away, Christian moved from the back of the car to the front so she'd have more room. Sophie continued to sleep with her head pressed into Bentley's shoulder. It felt so good to have her back with me. I knew our battles were far from over, but for now we had each other, and we'd get everything else figured out in time.

TWENTY ONE.
Sophie

I woke up and sat straight up, a gasp escaping my throat. I looked wildly around me. I was back in my own bed and in my home. Had it all been some horrible nightmare? When I glanced down at my stomach, and saw that it wasn't nearly as round as it had been, my heart stuttered in my chest. It hadn't been a nightmare. It was real. All of it was much too real.

My lip shook as I fought tears. I didn't want to cry. I wanted to be strong. Beau needed me to be strong.

Beau.

I had to find Beau.

I was his mother and he needed me.

I tried to remove myself from the bed, but found that I couldn't move. After everything I'd been through, my body was too tired.

I really did begin to cry then.

I felt like a sniveling baby. All I was doing was crying—at least it felt that way to me. I didn't like being…weak. I wanted to be a stronger person, and fight for what I believed in, but the way my body felt I wouldn't be fighting for a while. That didn't mean I wouldn't try though.

I braced my hands beside me and pushed myself into a sitting position. My body ached all over like I'd been tossed inside a dryer, spinning around uncontrollably. This was nothing like the exhaustion I'd experienced when I was pregnant with Beau. *Was*, keyword there, as in *not anymore*.

My breathing accelerated and I clutched at my chest.

I couldn't breathe and I felt like I was going to throw up. I tried to force oxygen into my lungs but it wasn't working. Was this what it felt like to have a panic attack? If so, I didn't like this one bit. I felt out of control of my body and I still couldn't *breathe*. My lungs made a strange wheezing noise as they tried to obtain oxygen, but it wasn't working.

Caeden burst into the bedroom and came running to my side. "Oh, Sophie, I meant to be here when you woke up. I'm so sorry." He took my face between his hands. "Breathe, baby. Just breathe like I am. Slowly…deep breath in…deep breath out."

I listened to his words, following what he said, and slowly I began to return to normal. My blood pressure lowered and I could breathe again.

"Better?" He asked, gazing at me with worried blue eyes. I'd been out of it when he found me and I wasn't sure how long I'd been sleeping, so this was the first time I was really seeing him since I'd been kidnapped. His hair was too long, falling into his eyes, and in the back it curled against the nape of his neck. His cheekbones were sharp and angular, telling me he'd lost weight. His eyes were sunken in and his lips had thinned. He looked like he'd aged tremendously in the past few months. Regardless, he was still the sexiest man I'd ever laid eyes on. "Better, Soph?" He repeated when I didn't answer him.

"Yeah," I nodded, placing my hand over one of his where it still rested against my cheek. I closed my eyes, memorizing the feel of him touching me, and soaking in his warmth. Gosh, I had really missed him. "I need…" I paused, unsure if I should continue.

"What do you need, baby? Whatever you need I'll give it to you." He spoke softly but fiercely.

I took a deep breath and let the words tumble from my mouth. "I need you to hold me. I need to feel you wrapped around me. I need you to make me realize that I'm not alone anymore, that you're real."

He swallowed thickly and his eyes shimmered. "I am here, Sophie," his fingers tangled in my hair, "and I'm not going anywhere."

A sob escaped my throat at those words. He enveloped me in his arms and laid us back on the bed. He held me close, front to front, and my hand rested against his chest where his heart beat proudly. We were both alive and we were here together, in each other's arms. We weren't whole though.

I sniffled, burrowing closer to him. His chin rested atop my head and his hands rubbed soothing circles on my back.

"I thought I might not ever get to hold you like this again," he admitted, his voice cracking. "I was scared out of my mind imagining what he was doing to you."

"I'm here now." I placed a light kiss against his collarbone. "We're together again—and that means we're unstoppable."

"And we're going to get our son back," he promised. "And we're going to end Travis and his mutants once and for all. This ends now. We're not going to keep living like this—always waiting for Travis to pop up again. He's going to die," he growled, "and so is anybody that stands with him."

"I agree," I whispered. "Caeden, I have to tell you what he told me." I drew random designs on his t-shirt, not wanting to look at him.

"It's bad, isn't it?" He sighed.

"Yeah," I frowned.

He sat up then, pulling me up with him, and took my chin between his fingers forcing me to look at him. "Just say it, Soph."

I swallowed thickly, trying to block out my memories of my time with Travis. I made myself tell him what I knew. "Travis said, that…that it was time shifters were on top. He and the elders…they're planning…" I paused, taking a steadying breath. "They want to take over the world. They want humans to know about shifters and bow down to them. He said that any human that disobeys them will be turned into a mutant—if they manage to survive the transformation." I pushed my hair out of my eyes, biting my lip nervously. "He never told me why he wanted Beau. He made it seem like he wanted me too. That he and I were going to rule the world. He kept calling Beau his child." Tears skated down my cheeks and I brushed them away. "Why would he want Beau? I don't understand! He's just a baby!" I cried.

Caeden pulled me back into his arms and stroked my hair, trying his best to comfort me.

"I don't know why he wants Beau either. My guess is that the elders want Beau, not Travis." His voice was surprisingly steady as he thought through what I had told him. "This is bad though. Based on the way they've disappeared, I'd say they're going to make their presence known to humans soon, and we have to stop them." His jaw was tight with tension and I hated that what I'd told him made him feel this way. But he had to know. We had a war on our hands.

His lips brushed against the top of my head before he pulled away and hopped lithely out of the bed. "Your parents are here, waiting to see you, and I really need to talk to Bentley. Are you okay to see them?"

I smoothed my fingers through my hair. "How scary do I look?" I didn't really care about my appearance, but after everything that happened I'd really like my parents to know I was okay and not look at me like I'd nearly died...which is what had happened. I didn't want either of them fussing over me. All I wanted was to put this behind me and find my son. I knew the elders and Travis were important too, but my baby was number one. I wrapped my arms around me, trying to hold myself together. I felt like my heart had been ripped from my body.

"Oh, Sophie," he rolled his eyes. "They don't care what you look like."

I nodded. "I want to see them."

"Stay in bed," he warned, pointing at me with a steady finger.

It was my turn to roll my eyes. "Trust me, I'm not moving for a week." Those words were truer than I wanted them to be. I wanted to be out there, hunting down Travis and the elders so I could get my son back, but I was too weak for that. Right now, I had to focus on rebuilding my strength. I knew Caeden would want to go after Travis soon, and I'd need to be on the top of my game, or he'd leave me behind. He'd have to restrain me to keep me from going, but I wouldn't put anything past Caeden if he thought it would keep me safe.

The door to the bedroom opened again and my mom poked her head inside. Her eyes filled with tears when she caught sight of me. "Oh, Sophie." She dove at me, but stopped herself from reaching out to hug me, for fear she might hurt me.

"I'm okay, mom. You can hug me," I assured her.

"Oh, thank God." She pulled me into her arms and held me tight. It was the kind of hug I'd received as a child when I'd fallen off my bike and hurt myself. It was the hug of a mother trying to repair all the broken pieces of her child. But some things can never be fixed, and I thought I might be one of those forever broken things. I'd been through *a lot*— which was quite the understatement—and I'd always been able to come out stronger because of it. But now, I hadn't just lost a piece of me. I'd lost a *part* of me. Beau. A hug couldn't fix the pain I was experiencing, no matter how much I might wish it would.

My mom's cries filled the room and her tears soaked the sweatshirt I was wearing.

"Mom, I'm okay. Honestly," I added. My voice was oddly flat and emotionless. I didn't like the sound of it. I was already going through the motions—saying things I knew they wanted to hear.

"You're not okay, baby girl," my dad spoke up from behind my mom. "Don't lie to us. We know you better than anyone."

I swallowed thickly at his words.

"It's okay to admit that not everything is fine, Sophie. We can help you. We can make it better," he continued.

"*Nothing* can make this better," my voice cracked. "Beau is *gone* and I might not ever see him."

"Baby girl, right now, you need to be optimistic." He stepped forward and lifted my hand off my mom's back— since she was still hugging me—and held it tightly in his. "You're Beau's momma and you need to believe that you're going to hold that child in your arms. He needs you to believe, baby girl."

"But it's so hard." I fought tears once more. You'd think my tear ducts would've dried up by now.

"I know it's hard, but that's life. Without the difficult things, we can't learn to appreciate the good things. We have to find the light in the darkness."

"I don't see any light." I bit my lip sharply, drawing blood, but I welcomed the short burst of pain and the slightly rusty tang of the blood on my tongue.

"There's light, baby girl, but you have to look closely. It might not be obvious at first, but there's always that glimmer of hope. Find it and cling to it, so it can keep you strong."

I soaked in his words, repeating them over and over again in my mind. I needed to find some hope to cling to, but I felt so defeated that hope seemed out of my reach.

My mom pulled back and took my face between her hands. She stared at me with a frown on her face. I wondered what she saw. I had yet to get a look at myself, but I was sure I was scary looking. My hair felt like it was sticking up around my head like Medusa's snake hair.

"You're going to be okay, Sophie," she said.

I closed my eyes, resisting the urge to tell her to shut up. I didn't want to be told that I'd be okay anymore. I knew I would—one day—but that didn't make it easier to hear. Right now, I wanted to wallow in my misery. I knew that wasn't the healthy thing to do, but I didn't care. I'd been stuck with Travis for *months*, I'd had my baby taken from me, and I'd nearly died. I think it was perfectly normal for me to want to feel unhappy.

"I know," I finally answered.

She kissed my forehead and then my dad stepped forward to hug me. He held me tighter than my mom had. I clung to him, wishing my parents' love for me could make everything better. Sometimes love isn't enough though, and we have to heal ourselves.

My dad released me and stepped back. He wiped beneath his eyes and looked away from me.

"Would you guys stay with me until Caeden gets back?" I pulled the covers up to my chin and sank against the fluffy pillows. I didn't want to be alone right now. Being left alone meant my thoughts were forced to wander back to why my womb was currently empty. I needed a distraction. Being surrounded by people, focusing on what they had to say, would force me away from thoughts that would leave me feeling ill.

"Of course, baby girl," my dad said, looking down at me like a small child who was sick in bed. "Do you want one of us to bring you something to eat or drink?"

The thought of food made me want to throw up. I was nowhere near ready to stomach anything. "I'd like some orange juice." I frowned. Orange juice. Something I'd craved while I was pregnant. This whole, not thinking unpleasant thoughts thing, was *so* not working out for me.

"I'll be right back." He forced a smile and I was left alone with my mom.

I untangled one of my arms from the blankets and patted the empty spot beside me on the bed. "You can sit down, mom."

She did so hesitantly, like I was a frightened bird that might take flight at any moment. I hated that she felt like she had to be so...gentle with me.

"Would you like me to braid your hair like I did when you were little? You always loved that," she whispered.

I closed my eyes, transported back to a time when I knew nothing about my heritage. I was just a girl. One who loved braids, wished unicorns were real, and thought my daddy would always be my prince charming. My how things had changed. I missed the innocence of childhood. If we could all stay that innocent the world would be a vastly different place.

"Yeah, I'd like that."

"Do you want to shower first?" She asked.

I frowned. I knew I was mess but I didn't see how I would have the strength to shower. "I can't. I'm too tired."

"I can help you."

What eighteen year old girl wants her mother to help her shower? Wait... "I'm not eighteen," I whispered. "I missed my own birthday."

"Oh, Sophie," my mom took me into her arms.

I wasn't crying, but I was in shock. That was something else Travis had taken away from me. I didn't even care that I had missed my birthday, I had way too many other things to be upset about, but it was the point of it.

I pushed her away, not wanting her comfort. "I can't believe I didn't remember my own birthday."

"Soph, you were with a sociopath. It's a miracle you're *alive*," she exclaimed.

"You don't understand," I whispered, staring off into space. "He keeps taking *everything* from me. Pretty soon, there will be nothing left."

I turned to face her and she swallowed thickly. "You have your *life*, Sophie. As long as you have that, you do have everything."

I shook my head. "I want that shower now."

She tilted her head to study me. She knew I was avoiding the conversation—that I didn't want to hear what she had to say.

"Alright," she pushed herself off the bed and into a standing position. She came around to me and helped me out of the bed.

It took me what felt like forever to make it to the bathroom and into the shower. My mom had to stand half in the shower to hold me up. I was so off balance that I kept teetering precariously. She helped me soap and rinse my hair. I tried my best to scrub my body, watching with a tortured expression as my dried blood and dirt descended down the drain.

Once I was clean, she helped me out of the shower and dried off my body. I'd long ago gotten over the embarrassment of my mother seeing me naked. I wasn't saying it wasn't awkward, but I didn't care anymore. I didn't care about a lot of things.

"Will you be okay to stand here while I get you some pajamas?" She asked.

I nodded, leaning against the wall for support.

She didn't take long. She returned with an old pair of pajamas and a loose t-shirt that belonged to Caeden. I winced as I lifted my arms above my head and she lowered the shirt down my body. I felt like I'd been kicked around by a bull. Without…without Beau, my body would heal faster, but after everything I'd been through it would still take some time.

She helped me back into bed and my dad was sitting in one of the chairs in the corner of the bedroom. I burrowed under the covers and my hand darted out to grab the glass of orange juice. I slurped at it greedily. The acidic juice burned my empty stomach, but it was still the best thing I had tasted in months. Travis had kept me fed, but everything had been basic and bland.

I finished off the orange juice and placed the empty glass on the table. My parents watched me with curious gazes. I think they kept waiting for the moment when I'd crack and completely splinter apart. I was trying my hardest to hold myself together. For now, Beau wasn't completely lost, so I was trying to do what my dad said and believe I'd hold my son in my arms.

"Do you still want me to braid your hair?" My mom asked.

I nodded, my head peeking out from the covers.

"You're going to have to sit up then," she laughed.

I reluctantly forced my body into a sitting position and turned so my back was to her. She already had a brush and hair ties. She sprayed detangler into my hair and began to brush out the tangled knots. I winced when she hit a particularly knotted spot.

"Sorry," she said.

"It's okay," I muttered, playing with a loose piece of thread on the blanket covering my legs.

Once my hair was tangle free, she braided it, draping the end over my shoulder.

"All done," she patted my back in a motherly gesture. I guessed no matter how old your children got, you couldn't stop yourself from still treating them like a child—not necessarily in a bad way.

"Thank you," I whispered, tucking myself back into my nest of blankets. "I-I want to go to sleep, but I still don't want you to leave. I-I need someone to be here, if I wake up." No way in hell did I want to experience another panic attack, if that meant I had to beg my parents to stay with me like I was still five years old and scared of the dark then so be it.

"We're not going anywhere," my mom assured me. "We won't leave until Caeden comes back."

"Thank you." By the time the two words left my mouth I was already asleep and I gladly let exhaustion consume me.

TWENTY TWO.
Sophie

I forced my tired and battered body out of the bed.

"Whoa, whoa, whoa!" Caeden jumped out of the bed and came running to my side. "Sophie, let me help you."

I swatted his reaching hand away. "I don't need your help," I grumbled. "I'm perfectly capable of walking to the bathroom by myself."

"Sophie—"

"Leave me alone." I shuffled past him at a turtles pace, but he let me. I'd been home for three days and he barely let me do anything on my own. This was me asserting that I was okay. I was independent by nature and I was sick of having to ask people for help. I needed to prove to myself and to Caeden that I was *okay*. I was getting better, and soon I'd be ready to hunt down Travis. When I got my hands on him...well, it wouldn't be pretty.

I finished in the bathroom and made my way back into the bedroom. Caeden shadowed me, like he was waiting for me to fall over.

"I'm fine," I snapped with an angry bite to my tone.

"Sophie," he said my name sternly, "accepting help doesn't make you weak, it makes you smart."

"I'm sick of your help," I spat, heading for the door, not the bed. He jumped in front of me and used his body to block the door. My nostrils flared in anger. "Caeden, *move*. I refuse to sit in this room for one more second. In order to get better, I need to get up and move around. Lying here doing nothing isn't helping me. It's making me worse. Can't you see that?" I spread my arms wide in exasperation.

He rubbed his jaw and moved aside. He swung the door open and motioned me out. "Fine, but I'm helping you down the stairs. Don't even think about arguing with me."

"Whatever," I rolled my eyes. His overprotectiveness was grading on my last nerve. Don't get me wrong, I loved the man with all my heart, but it was getting to be a bit much.

I stepped into the hallway outside our bedroom. A ladder sitting outside one of the guest bedrooms caught my eye. I headed that way out of curiosity. What was he up to?

"Sophie, no—"

His warning was too late though. I'd already opened the door.

I dropped to my knees as an indescribable pain ripped through my body. It was like I was being torn apart from the inside.

The room…it was a nursery. *Beau's* room. A room he might never come home to. The room was perfect in every way. It looked like something straight out of a magazine but it was missing something very important—a baby.

I couldn't believe I'd forgotten this was his room. It was like I was purposely torturing myself.

"Sophie—" Caeden reached for me, but I shrugged off his touch.

"No." The word left my mouth sharply. "I need to see this."

I slowly came to my feet and stepped forward into the room.

While I'd been gone, Caeden had been preparing for our return. Little did he know that I'd come home without our baby. I guess he had needed to hope though and I couldn't blame him for that.

The walls were a pale brown color—not the typical blue, green, or yellow you saw in a baby's room—and it was the color I had picked out and was having painted the day I was taken. The furniture was a dark wood. The bed things *were* blue. A pretty white chair, large enough for two people to sit in, was near the bed with a little stuffed animal dog sitting on it. A fluffy white rug covered the wood floors. It would have been the perfect place to sit with the baby.

"It's perfect," I whispered, reaching up to wipe away tears from beneath my eyes.

"I didn't mean for you to see this." Caeden said from somewhere behind me.

187

I shrugged. "I'm glad I did." My breath was shaky as I fought a breakdown, but I wasn't lying. I was glad I saw this. Beau might not ever come home, but I could imagine what could have been.

I closed my eyes, envisioning a squirming baby in my arms.

Caeden came up behind me and wrapped his arms around me. His chin rested on my shoulder and he held me tightly, like he believed his strength alone would hold me together.

"I'm okay," I assured him. "Really."

"Beau's going to come home to us, baby. He's going to sleep in this room and grow up in this house. He's going to play games and call us mom and dad. And one day, when you're ready, we'll give him a little brother or sister. We're going to have it all, Sophie."

My tongue flicked out to wet my lips. "I hope you're right."

"I am." His lips brushed softly against my neck. It wasn't really a kiss, more of a caress.

I extracted myself from his arms and turned around to face him. "I can't believe you managed to do all this with everything that was going on and the way you must have been feeling."

"It was awful," he swallowed thickly, "but I know what I felt was nowhere near close to what you were feeling."

I reached up, placing my hand against his stubbled cheek. "We've both been through a lot. Our experiences may have been different, but that doesn't make them any less painful."

"You're so right." He smoothed a finger down my cheek. The simple touch sent a shiver down my spine. Our time together, from the moment we'd met, had been full of good and bad things. But I wouldn't trade those bad things for anything. Everything we'd been through had made us stronger people and therefore a stronger couple.

I looked behind me at the baby's room once more. "Let's go."

* * *

I was ready.

Caeden didn't believe I was ready. But I was. My injuries had healed and I felt *normal* again. Well, as normal as I could feel. I was still emotionally drained from losing Beau, but physically I was great. I wasn't going to sit around anymore. I was better and I was going to find my son so I could *end* this. If Caeden didn't want to come with me, then he could stay behind here with his tail tucked between his legs. I didn't need him to do this. I knew I was strong enough to take on Travis. Now, add in the elders and mutants, and I'd probably get myself killed, but it was a risk I was willing to take. I was a mama wolf now without her cub, and I was going to get my baby back. It didn't matter what I had to do. Travis had messed with me one too many times and this would be the last.

"I'm going to get our baby back," I stated, standing in the doorway of Caeden's office. "You can come with me or not, I don't care, but I'm going to find him."

The color drained from his face. "Sophie, we have no idea where Travis and the elders are hiding out. You can't just *leave!* We need a plan!" He looked at me like I'd lost my mind, which was quite possible.

"Plans have done nothing but get us in trouble. I'm sick of strategizing only to have it blow up in our faces. Our plans never work out, so why bother?" I questioned, crossing my arms over my chest. I knew I was being a bitch, but I didn't care. It was true. Our plans had been no good. We always ended up going in blind anyway.

He smacked his hand roughly against the wooden top of his desk. The sound caused me to jump. "I understand that, and it makes sense, but we still don't know where Travis is!"

189

"I can find him," I stepped into the room, determination ringing in my voice. "He has our *son*, Caeden. It's called a mother's instinct. I'll be able to find my baby." I placed my hand against my heart, where a significant portion was missing where my love for Beau had been cut out.

He shook his head, his hair falling into his eyes.

Before he could speak I continued. "I don't care what you have to say, Caeden. I really don't. I'm going. So either you're with me or you're not. I'm ending this."

"God, Sophie," he scrubbed his hands over his face and letting out an animal like growl, "you know I'm with you. We're stronger together. But we're so unprepared."

I so wanted to punch him in the face right now. "Plans and preparedness have never helped us before, so why would now be any different?"

He sighed. "Alright. Let's do this. I'll call the pack."

* * *

We were back at the elders headquarters where I'd been held. We were all in our wolf forms. I smelled around, looking for a trail. I know no one had found anything before, but I was convinced I could find something.

I sniffed around, following the lingering scent that I knew belonged to Travis. The other wolves trailed behind me and Caeden was close by my side.

I headed deeper and deeper into the woods, and like they'd described to Caeden the scent stopped suddenly. It literally just ended and didn't continue in any direction. I pawed the ground, a whine escaping me.

My act of pawing the ground disturbed the leaves and debris, revealing a trapped door in the ground. I barked in elation. Caeden switched to his human form and lifted the latch. It opened into what looked like a wine cellar. I descended into the depths behind Caeden who had already switched back to wolf form. I looked around at the bottles lining the walls. My guess was that this place had held illegal alcohol in the prohibition era. Only where the cellar wall had once ended, the cement blocks had been broken down, littering the ground and a hallway had been hollowed out.

My heart was racing. This was it. This would lead us to Beau. I knew it. He was close.

The hallway was narrow so Caeden and I couldn't walk side by side, we all had to fall into a single file line. I didn't like that fact one bit. If something attacked from in front of Caeden, he was completely alone and none of us would be able to help him. The makeshift hallway dipped down, leading further beneath the surface of the earth.

My sides brushed the walls and dirt coated my fur. Insects crawled along the dirt floor and if I'd been in my human form I would have been grossed out, but as a wolf I didn't care.

The hallway continued on and on. I knew we'd walked at least two miles and there was no sign of anyone or that we were reaching the end of the tunnel. I was beginning to feel claustrophobic, and feared this had been a trap and that we'd be stuck down here until we ran out of oxygen and perished. Morbid thoughts, but with someone like Travis, it was a completely realistic assumption. I filled my mind with thoughts of Beau so that I didn't freak out, and it did help.

The tunnel made a sharp right turn and we began to ascend. I saw light from somewhere up ahead and I began to panic. If we were coming to the end of the tunnel, then Travis wasn't here, and I had no idea what would greet us once we reached the surface. Travis could still be there, wherever there was, but chances were he was long gone and my child with him. How would I manage to go on knowing my child was alive and well, but trapped with a sociopath like Travis?

I see light ahead. Caeden said. *We need to be prepared in case they're waiting for us.*

His words made my heart race a mile a minute in my chest. Adrenaline was already coursing through my veins. I was ready for whatever greeted us. My jaw snapped together and my lips pulled back to show off my sharp teeth. This mama wolf was ready to kill whoever stood in the way of her and her child.

Before we reached the opening, Caeden stopped. *Brace yourselves.*

He surged forward, running as fast as his legs would carry him. I was quick to follow, close enough to him that if I wanted I could bite into his legs. Bentley, who was behind me, was on my heels as well.

Our pack shot out of the tunnel opening like bullets out of a gun. We were nothing but streaks of fur.

And we weren't alone.

There were mutants everywhere, and they were surrounding a house.

I didn't wait for orders. I jumped forward, smacking into the nearest mutant and pushing her to the ground. She wrapped her hands around my arms and squeezed, but I felt nothing. The adrenaline had made me numb. I lowered my mouth and bit into her throat. Blood spurted everywhere, into my mouth, onto my fur, and all over the ground. The light left her eyes and her hands fell slack at her sides.

I didn't wait around. I struck out at the next closest mutant, jumping onto his back and like with the girl, I bit into his throat. My teeth cut right through the muscle and his severed head fell to the ground. I gagged on the sickly tasting blood, trying to spit it out.

Everyone was fighting and bodies were littering the ground. Luckily, every body my eyes landed on was that of a mutant.

We were tearing them apart so quickly that their numbers had dwindled substantially. I had been right to say we didn't need a plan. Attacking without though, allowed us to act on instinct alone.

I caught sight of one mutant trying to sneak away towards to the house. I sprinted after him, jumping on his back and knocking him to the ground. My claws dug into his back, ripping and tearing. He screamed and the sound filled me with a sick joy. I shouldn't have been enjoying myself— the mutants couldn't help what they were. Travis had turned them into these monsters and they'd once been human. But they were helping him and I was so blinded by rage that I didn't care.

I moved on from that mutant to another, and then another. I quickly lost count of how many I'd killed. More kept appearing and we continued to kill them.

No more than two minutes had passed till they were all dead and nothing stood in our way of the house.

Told you we didn't need a plan. I told Caeden.

Seems that way. He responded. *But this is nowhere near over yet.*

We ran forward, towards the house located what seemed a half a mile ahead of us. I kept expecting another mutant to jump out at us, but there was nothing but an empty field. As we got closer, I decided the house was actually sort of pretty. It was two stories with cheery yellow siding and white shutters. Each window even had a flower box. It wasn't the kind of place you expected Travis to hide out in. I'd thought we'd find him in a cave or some run down dilapidated house with the roof caving in. Certainly not this. It looked...homey.

We reached the front door and Caeden told us to stop.

We need to split up so we can cover all sides so they can't escape out the back or from a side window. Bentley and Bryce, you're with Sophie and me. Garrett, I want you to lead a group around back. Christian, you take a group to the right side of the house. Jeremy, you take a group to the left side. Everyone understand?

There were no objections and Caeden took that as enough of an answer.

He switched to his human form and turned the knob.

It didn't open.

He shifted back into a wolf and warned, *Get back.*

Everyone was quick to move out of his way. He backed up and braced himself. He ran forward as fast as he could and smashed the door in. Wood splinters flew everywhere and I ducked down to avoid getting nailed in the eye by one.

Bentley, Bryce, and I followed Caeden into the house. The two guys were quick to move behind me so that Caeden and I were in the lead. Some instinct told them to stay out of my way. Smart boys.

Caeden and I followed the scent of Travis upstairs and to a room at the very end of the hallway. We stopped outside, looking at each other carefully, preparing ourselves for what we might be met with.

With a nod, Caeden pushed his wolf body against the door and the hinges broke with the pressure.

I was not expecting the sight that met us.

The room was decorated as a nursery. The walls were yellow with ducks on them and a white crib sat in the middle of the room. There was even a changing table. It was what you'd expect to see in any home with a baby. What you didn't expect though, was Travis sitting in the corner in a rocking chair, with my baby in his arms, as he fed him from a bottle.

"Shhh," Travis whispered, "you'll wake the baby."

Holy crap. What was this freak show? This had to be the strangest thing I had ever seen. It made no sense. And where were the elders?

Bentley, Bryce, look for the elders. My tone brooked no argument and they quickly left us. I sunk down, stalking forward, my growl filling the room.

I had to figure out how to get to Travis without hurting the baby, and that was easier said then done. My hackles rose and my lips pulled back from my mouth, exposing my teeth. Teeth I wanted to sink into every part of his body and rip him apart.

"Ah, Sophie," he turned his head, studying me, "I'm surprised to see you alive."

I couldn't resist it. I shifted to my human form and Caeden darted in front of me, ready to protect me if he needed to.

"Why did you try to kill me?" I asked through gritted teeth. "You made it seem like we were going to be a family." I pointed at him and then myself. "What changed?"

He removed the bottle from Beau's mouth and set it aside. He lifted the baby to his shoulder and patted his back, like he was burping him. "It was obvious that you couldn't accept our plan. You would've been a weakness. Besides, this little guy is the one I really wanted." He lowered the baby and cradled him in his arms. He reached out with a finger, rubbing Beau's cheek as he cooed at him.

"What's so special about my son?" I asked.

Travis ignored me, playing with the baby. Caeden's growl forced his attention back to me. "You'll find out soon enough."

I swallowed thickly. I didn't like the sound of that.

"Tell me now," I whispered. "I want to know why Beau is so important."

"Beau? Is that the name you're going with? Pretty crappy if you ask me," he shrugged. "I've been calling him Laurence."

"You named my baby?!" I shrieked, the high decibel making the glass on the windows shake. Beau began to cry.

"Look what you've done, Sophie." Travis shook his head and began to comfort the baby. *I* should have been the one comforting him. Not Travis. This wasn't okay with me at all. But I still didn't know what to do. Attacking Travis would result in hurting Beau, and Travis was smart enough to know that. He held the advantage here. "You should really keep your voice down. Laurence is sensitive to loud noises."

"His. Name. Is. Beau." I seethed, my fists clenched at my sides. I'm sure my face was turning bright red with anger. I was so pissed off it wasn't even funny. At this point I was pretty sure I could kill Travis with my bare hands alone—that was how angry I was.

"Once again," he kissed the baby's cheek, "Beau is a really shitty name and you should reconsider. The Prince deserves a strong name."

"Prince?" I swallowed thickly, raising a brow in confusion.

"Yes, *the* Prince."

"The Prince?" I was so confused with Travis' gibberish. For once couldn't he just spit out whatever it was he had to say?

He rolled his eyes. "Oh, sweet Sophie, you are so incredibly dumb. Long ago, back when humans were just beginning to stand on two legs, the Book of Legends was born and it foretold of a Prince. A wolf prince, born to the two most powerful Alpha's to ever grace our shifter history, and blah, blah, blah. I think they got that part wrong though. I mean, y'all are the crappiest Alphas I know, but whatever. The elders said it was you guys." He shrugged, glancing back down at the baby. "The firstborn son of these Alphas, you two," he pointed at Caeden and then me, as if we needed clarification, "would have powers unlike *any* shifter out there. His powers are far advanced from ours. He can run faster, see better, he's stronger, and even as a wee wittle baby," his voice went all high pitched and squeaky, "he can shift."

"What? That's not possible," I gasped.

"That's what I meant when I said you'd find out soon enough. Since he's so small, he can't control his shifts so they happen sporadically. One time he didn't quite transform all the way and he was half in human for and half wolf. I think I got a picture on my phone. It was *hilarious!*"

I shook my head at the strangeness of the conversation. Travis was speaking to me like we were old friends having a chat over coffee—not like he'd tried to kill me *twice*.

He was a strange dude.

"Alright, so he can transform," I said, "that doesn't explain why you want my son."

Travis chuckled, the sound sharp and grating, sending shivers down my spine. "Did you miss the part where I said he was powerful? Y'all are dumb, but even you two should have figured out by now that I crave *power*." He stood, stalking forward. He surprised me by stopping to lay the baby in the crib. I let out a sigh of relief I hoped he didn't notice. We could attack now without worrying about hurting the baby.

197

"But you told me that you and the elders want to expose yourself to humans, that you want to start a war. How is a *baby* going to help you accomplish that?"

Travis shrugged. "He might not be able to help us now, but kids grow, and I can hone his powers to my advantage." He shoved his hands in his pockets, the picture of ease.

"To your advantage?" I whispered, picking up on the fact that what he said had no mention of the elders.

Travis smiled slowly, his grin reminding me of a villain in a comic book. "Yes, *my* advantage. After you delivered the baby, I didn't need them anymore because I had everything I needed. Let me tell you, they *begged* for their lives. It was pathetic really. So you don't need to worry about them anymore. I've already taken care of them for you. And no more elders mean I can create a whole new order. I will be King and your son will be the Prince. And you two will be dead."

"I'm not going anywhere," I said slowly, shaking my head. "And I think that you'll find a wolf protecting her cub is *very* hard to kill."

"Oooh, she wants a fight," Travis grinned. "I'll give you a fight, sweet Sophie, and in the end you'll be *begging* me to end your life, and I'm going to drag it out as long as possible. I'll make sure it's extra painful too and that your mate here gets to watch," he nodded at Caeden who stood in front of me in his wolf form, growling.

"Bring. It. On." I said the words slowly and carefully, staring him down the whole time. I wanted him to know that I wasn't afraid of him. I had a child to protect, and that erased all my fears for myself.

"Consider it brought."

With a roar, his body exploded in midair and a white wolf stood in front of Caeden.

I shifted too and jumped over Caeden's body. I sank my teeth into Travis' shoulder and he yelped in pain. But he was bigger than me and easily shook off my hold. I went flying through the air and smacked into one of the walls. It hurt something fierce and there was a dent left behind in the wall, but I surged forward like I had felt nothing.

Teeth. Claws. Growls. I didn't know who was who and I sincerely hoped I didn't hurt Caeden by accident. I was unstoppable in that moment, my adrenaline alone giving me a strength I didn't know I possessed, not to mention the strength of a mother protecting her child.

Blood coated my mouth and tongue with a rusty taste. It was disgusting, but my mouth was my best weapon. My teeth tore into Travis back leg and blood spurted across my face. He cried out in pain as my teeth ripped through flesh and muscle. That was definitely going to hurt like a bitch and slow him down.

Good job she-wolf. Caeden said.

My jubilation didn't last long though. Travis smacked into me, knocking me off balance. I fell to the ground and he climbed on top of me. His paws pressed painfully into my unprotected belly. He dug his claws in, shredding my skin like I had done with his leg. His lifeless black eyes gazed down at me. He felt no sympathy for what he was doing. Killing was second nature for him.

Suddenly he was knocked off of me and I rolled over to see him grappling with Caeden. I forced air into my lungs, wincing at the pain in my abdomen. A wheezing noise escaped me and blood began to fill my throat. I wasn't a doctor but I was pretty sure he'd punctured one of my lungs. This was bad. But I wasn't going to let it keep me from taking the son of a bitch down. I forced myself to my feet. My vision was blurry from blood loss and I swayed precariously. I pushed myself forward, one foot at a time as Caeden grappled with Travis' white form. I wanted—no, I *needed*—to be the one to kill Travis. I knew Caeden wanted the honor, but this was my fight, not his.

I inserted my body between Caeden and Travis'. Caeden let out a howl of protest.

I need to do this. I told him.

He didn't have a reply because he understood.

Travis and I were both weak from fighting, but I had something he didn't. What was that you might ask? I had everything. A husband, a child, family, friends, a *life*. Travis, well, he had nothing to live for.

With a renewed strength I sunk my teeth into his throat. He screamed—and a wolf's scream was nothing like that of a human. It was an unnatural sound. Wolves aren't supposed to scream. I bit into his body in different places, ripping straight through the flesh, and watching as his blood seeped over the floor. The sticky red substance coated my muzzle and paws, but I didn't care, because I was watching Travis' black eyes fade to a dull gray as his life left him. His body shimmered, transforming back into that of a human. Pieces of his skin hung in shreds and blood trickled from the corner of his mouth. He was dead.

Dead.

Finally.

I shifted back to my human form, a cry tearing from my throat. He was actually dead. I had done it. I had killed Travis Grimm. Not Caeden. Me. I'd been the one to kill him. He couldn't bother us ever again. It was over. It was finally over.

Caeden shifted too, placing his hand on the bare skin of my back. I was hunched over, fighting tears of happiness, and struggling to breathe. My lungs were slowly repairing themselves and I felt a slight stinging pain as they knitted back together.

"Are you okay?" Caeden asked. His voice seemed too loud in the suddenly silent room.

"I've never been better," I answered honestly. My words were true. For the first time in a year I could breathe a sigh of relief because it was *over*. Travis was dead, which meant he could never torment us again—except in the memories that would probably always haunt me. But we wouldn't have to look over our shoulders anymore. We didn't have to live in fear. We could finally be normal, and go back to being Caeden and Sophie. Well, Caeden and Sophie plus Beau.

I came to my feet and ventured hesitantly towards the crib. I gazed down at the tiny bundle. Bright blue eyes—the same blue as his fathers—gazed up at me. Fluffy downy soft brown hair cover the top of his head and his lips were heart shaped. His nose was teeny tiny. Everything about him was perfect.

"Hi, Beau," I gasped in awe. "I'm your mommy."

I hadn't had a chance to grasp the profoundness of that word with everything that had happened. Mommy. I was a mom. This tiny breakable human was mine. I would watch him grow up and nurture him into a young man and scold him when he did something wrong.

He was mine. A piece of me that was precious and irreplaceable. I reached down, scooping him into my arms. He was so small, fitting perfectly into the curve of my arms like a football. I lowered my head, pressing kisses to the top of his head. He made a cute little noise and burrowed close to me. He was the cutest baby I had ever seen in my entire life, and he was mine.

"I love him so much," I gasped, letting him wrap his tiny fingers around one of mine. I never wanted to let him go. I wanted to hold him in my arms forever so no harm could ever come his way. I would always protect him, but hopefully he would never need protecting like this ever again.

I kissed his small nose and sighed. I knew I had to let go of him. Caeden deserved to hold him too. I certainly didn't make this cute thing by myself. Caeden had played a very important role and he'd been just as worried as I had been.

"Here," I adjusted the baby so I could hold him out to Caeden, "hold your son."

Caeden's eyes shimmered with unshed tears at my words. He took the baby from me and gazed down at him with the same expression I was sure I had worn.

"Hey, Beau," Caeden bounced the baby in his arms. "It's nice to finally meet you. I've been really worried about you."

"Whoa."

Caeden and I both startled at the new voice and looked to the doorway to see Bentley and Bryce standing there. I averted my eyes at their nakedness—maybe one day I'd get used to shifters running around naked, but today was not that day.

"He's dead," Bryce continued. "You really killed him."

"Of course he's dead," Bentley smacked the back of Bryce's head, rolling his eyes at his idiocy.

"Hey, Travis is crazy. It was reasonable for me to think he might kill them. I'm just saying." He shrugged.

"God, you're an idiot," Bentley shook his head. "Anyway, sorry to break up your happy little reunion here," Bentley pointed at Caeden and I with the baby, "but you're going to want to see this."

My stomach plummeted. What could it be now?

Caeden handed Beau back to me and we followed the guys down to a basement. It was dark with no light. A dank musty smell filled the air, but another scent was stronger— that of decay.

Since there was no light it took my eyes a moment to adjust to the dark.

"Oh my God," I gasped, fighting my gag reflex.

The bodies of the elders were scattered along the floor of the basement. Their bodies weren't whole though. They were ripped into pieces and some of those pieces looked like they'd been chewed on. "Oh my God," I repeated. "He was eating them."

I had never been so repulsed in all my life. I'd heard of such things, but seeing it firsthand…it was definitely the most disturbing thing I had ever seen. I held Beau tightly in one arm and used my free hand to cover my nose and mouth.

"Is…Is Gram among them?" I closed my eyes, my breath shaking as I waited for their answer. Gram was an elder, but I knew there was no way she'd been involved with Travis. That didn't mean he had spared her when he decided to kill the other elders though.

I heard shuffling and assumed the guys were looking through the body parts, looking for any sign of Gram. Wow, what a disturbing thought. I hadn't seen Gram in—well, forever it seemed like—she hadn't been there when I woke up and she wasn't with us when we came here. There was a very real possibility that she was dead.

"She's not here," Caeden finally said after an agonizing minute of waiting.

"Oh, thank God," I breathed, letting my eyes open. Relief flooded my body. Gram was okay. *Everything* was okay now. "Hey…" I paused. "Do you guys smell that?" I asked.

Caeden tilted his head back, sniffing the air. His eyes widened. "Smoke."

Holy crap, the house was on fire.

We ran for the stairs and back up to the main level of the house. The smoke was thick up here, but the fire seemed to be coming from the back, so we were able to make it to the front door. We burst outside, letting the clean air flood our lungs. I was still wheezing slightly, but my lungs had almost repaired themselves.

I looked Beau over, making sure he was okay. He looked up at me with confused blue eyes and then coughed. As he coughed though, he transformed from a baby human to a wolf cub.

"Oh. My. God. Travis wasn't lying," I gasped in surprise.

"What the hell is that thing?" Bentley exclaimed.

"Beau," I answered simply. "Apparently he's special."

"Obviously," Bentley gasped.

"Whoa, that's cool!" Bryce shouted. "I want one!"

Caeden snorted. "A baby? You want a baby?"

Bryce shrugged. "Well, when you put it that way, no. But look, he's so cute and fluffy and he's gray like you."

Caeden wore a proud smirk. "That's my boy."

Bentley shook his head. "We better get the others and see why the hell the house is on fire."

I frowned down at Beau. I was scared to follow the guys in case we were walking into a dangerous situation. I couldn't fight with Beau in my arms, but staying here by myself wasn't a safe option either.

With a pop, Beau shifted back into his human form.

"Y'all lead the way."

The guys shifted into their wolf form and I followed behind them.

When we reached the back of the house we found all the wolves we'd left behind outside. No one seemed hurt, but there were more mutant bodies lying on the ground. A door to what looked an underground cellar—much like the one we'd traveled through—was open and that's where the mutants had come from and where the fire was burning.

I looked around to see if anyone was still fighting, but all the mutants were dead and it looked every member of our pack was safe. Thank God for that. I didn't think my conscious could handle any more deaths of our friends and family.

A cry escaped my throat—a cry of relief. We had our son back and the threat of a war with humans was over. We could all move on and live normal lives—well, as normal of a life as you can live when you're a shifter.

Nolan's tiger formed stalked forward and I knew he was communicating with Caeden. The wolves all listened intently to whatever Caeden was saying. I could tell when they learned that Travis was dead, because if it was possible for wolves to dance, that was definitely what they were doing.

Caeden shifted back to his human form and grabbed my face between his hands. Before I could blink he kissed me soundly. The wolves howled in happiness. He pulled back, smoothing his thumb over my lip. "Let's go home, she-wolf."

TWENTY THREE.
Sophie

"And this is your room," I cooed to Beau as I opened the door to his nursery.

"Sophie, he's barely two weeks old, I don't think he needs a whole tour of the house," Caeden chuckled behind me.

"Shut up," I grumbled. "If I want to give our son a tour of our house, I will."

We'd only been home long enough to shower and dress and I'd reluctantly had to relinquish Beau to Caeden to do that. But now he was all mine and I was never letting him go. I'd heard people say that holding a baby all the time would make them clingy, but I didn't care. I'd almost lost Beau, and if I didn't look at him at least once every five minutes then I was convinced he wasn't real.

Caeden and I had given him a bath and I'd dressed him in a cute blue sleeper with monkeys on it. I'd also wrapped him in a pretty white blanket so he currently looked like a little burrito. I found myself constantly staring at him, trying to memorize his features.

I sat in the big white chair with him in my arms, and Caeden squeezed in beside me.

"Do you know the legend Travis was talking about? The one about the Prince?"

Caeden nodded. "Only, it was never in the Book of Legends. He lied about that. It was just a story parents told their children. It was called The Wolf Prince. My mom used to tell it to me and Bryce to help us sleep when we were little."

"But it's true," I stated. "Beau can shift."

"That he can," Caeden shook his head, staring off into space. "You know, they always said that the most powerful wolves always have a full moon on their birthday that they transform. That happened to both of us, then we're mates, *and* Alphas...maybe those three factors coming together resulted in Beau," he shrugged, reaching out to hold the baby's hand. Beau's clenched fist looked incredibly tiny resting in Caeden's open palm. "I know it's a long shot, but it's the only thing I can think of," he shrugged again.

"The story...what did it say about him?" I questioned.

"Man, it's been a long time since I heard that story. I'm not sure if I really remember. Basically, like Travis said, the wolf prince is stronger and more powerful than the typical shifter. But what he didn't say, is that the wolf prince is extremely compassionate. He's supposed to bring peace to all shifters...to unite us all together."

My brows furrowed together in confusion. "But...I didn't know there was any animosity between different types of shifters. I mean, you're friends with Nolan and he's a tiger, so..." I trailed off.

"Sophie, where we are there aren't that many groups of shifters. You have us, what was the Grimm pack, and Nolan's family," he ticked each off on his fingers. "Most are up north and to the west. It's easier for them to blend in. And while there's not a lot of hostility like what we've had to deal with from Travis, there is a rift. I guess little man is so supposed to repair that," he flicked a finger against Beau's nose. "But it is just a story. Who knows what we can expect? For now, I say we take everything one day at a time. We'll cross those bridges when we get to them."

"When did you get so smart?" I laughed, beaming up at him.

"Since always," he smirked, kissing me. I had missed moments like these—moments when we were just normal Caeden and Sophie and we didn't have to stress about Travis.

It was hard to believe, that after more than year and watching our friends die, it was over. Travis was dead and he was never coming back.

We'd stuck around to watch the house burn down and when it had completely crumbled to ash, I'd felt so...relieved. I was finally at peace. We didn't have to constantly look over our shoulders, wondering when Travis would make an appearance. He was really and truly gone, and we had nothing to worry about anymore. It all seemed so surreal. It had been a long exhausting journey to get to this point though. People had died and our lives had forever been altered, but it really had come to an end. I'd never forget the ones we'd lost though. We'd been lucky not to lose anyone this time, but we hadn't been as lucky in the past. I missed Logan something fierce, but without his sacrifice I'd have died and I would've never had the chance to hold my son. Gazing down at Beau, I knew it was all worth it, and I'd go through everything again and again for him. He was worth everything. And in the end, we had avenged Logan's death and the deaths of the others who were no less important. Even Leslee Grimm, Travis' mother, had gotten the justice she deserved.

The door to Beau's nursery opened and we looked up to find Nolan standing there.

"Hi," he said, clearing his throat awkwardly.

"Hey," I smiled. "What do you need?"

"I thought I should let you guys know that everyone is here," he scratched his jaw.

"Everyone?" Caeden questioned.

"Everyone," Nolan nodded. "They want to see the baby, and Lucinda brought cake. Let me tell you, it took all my strength not to steal that delicious looking cake and hide in my room stuffing my face."

I laughed, shaking my head. "Tell them we'll be right down."

Nolan nodded, leaving the door open behind him.

I looked down at Beau, sleeping peacefully in my arms, then up at my husband. I was so full of love I thought I might burst. "I want you to know, that you're worth it, Caeden." His eyes fluttered closed at my words and a sigh escaped his lips. "I know you think that if I'd never met you, my life would've been happier, but you're wrong. *You* make my life worth living. The both of you," I placed a kiss on the baby's head. "I never want you to doubt how I feel. Not for a minute." I leaned over and kissed him softly on the lips.

"I love you, Soph," he whispered, his eyes swimming with the love he'd just declared. Having someone look at you like that—with such pure love—it was the best feeling in the world. I wished everyone could find their mate, that one person they belonged with more than anyone else, so that they could experience a special kind of love. The love you read about in fairytales and hope you'll find, but so rarely do. But I'd found it, and we'd had to fight for it, but I wouldn't have it any other way. It made us appreciate each other even more.

He pressed his lips to mine, kissing me deeply.

Beau began to squirm in my arms and we were forced to break apart. We looked down at him and his eyes were open, his nose wiggling.

"Did you not like Daddy kissing Mommy?" Caeden chuckled. "You better get used to it. I love her and plan on giving her lots of kisses."

Beau wiggled again, making a face that wrinkled his forehead.

"Look at that, he's already a mommy's boy and doesn't want me to talk about you. I see how it is son."

I smiled at Caeden and then Beau. My little family was finally complete. And our big extended family was waiting for us downstairs.

"Well, Beau," I tickled his cheek, "I guess it's time for you to meet the rest of your family."

Caeden helped me up from the chair and then worried over me as I walked down the steps with Beau in my arms.

"Honestly, Caeden, I'm not going to drop him. You don't need to walk like that in front of me," I grumbled.

"Sorry," his cheeks flushed and he turned around.

We found everyone waiting for us in the family room. I ran straight into Gram's arms, bursting into tears.

Beau made a quiet sound of protest at nearly being squished to death and I felt like the worst mom ever. Hopefully I'd get the hang of this whole parenting thing soon. Obviously I wasn't one of those people who had a kid and seemed to automatically know the right thing to do all the time.

"Let me see that precious baby boy," Gram cooed, reaching her arms out for Beau.

I didn't want to release the baby, but I figured I better get used to it. Everyone wanted to meet the baby.

I handed Beau to Gram and smiled as she beamed at the baby. "He's perfect, Sophie," she whispered.

"I know," I smiled proudly. I knew I was like all parents, thinking their kid was the cutest and smartest baby to ever grace the face of the earth, but I didn't care. I'd almost lost Beau, and that made him even more special.

Despite the fact that Beau was only a newborn, I already found myself worrying about his future. I wondered what kind of responsibility he'd have to face with his special ability to shift already. But like Caeden said, we'd cross that bridge when we came to it.

For now, I was going to live every day with a smile on my face, because the war was over before it even started, I had the best baby and husband in the whole world, and I had my family to keep me strong. I couldn't ask for anything else.

"What are you thinking?" Caeden whispered in my ear, wrapping his arms around me from behind.

"I was just thinking about how thankful I am, for everything." I closed my eyes, letting his warmth envelope me in comfort. "Travis is gone so we don't have to worry about him anymore, and we have these awesome people surrounding us. Our life is pretty amazing," I smiled as his lips brushed my jaw.

"You bet it is, and its barely even started."

EPILOGUE. SIX YEARS LATER.

Sophie

"Beau!" I yelled. "Do *not* shoot Nerf gun bullets at your little brother! It's not nice! Now apologize!" I scolded my oldest son. He was going through a stage where all he did was torment his little brother. Poor Grant was only three and didn't understand what was going on.

"Sorry, mommy," Beau dropped his plastic gun to the ground and looked up at me with wide blue eyes.

"Say you're sorry to Grant," I repeated, "and then give him a hug."

Beau sighed but did as I had asked. "Sorry, Grant."

"Now hug," I pointed a finger at my sons.

Beau wrapped his arms around Grant in a hug. Grant placed a loud kiss on Beau's cheek.

"Ew! Mommy! Grant got spit on me!" Beau screamed, swiping his arm across his cheek.

I sighed. This was what my life had become. Referee to two hard-headed little boys, and the newest edition, our little Lucy. She was only two months old and even cuter than her brothers. She was already her daddy's little princess. I loved seeing Caeden with her. It made my heart do a little dance.

Ignoring Beau's comment, I said, "Now boys, everyone's going to be here in just a few minutes, so I want you to be on your best behavior."

The boys both saluted me like they were little soldiers.

Caeden came out the back door with Lucy strapped to his chest in one of those holder things.

"Here, take her so I can start the grill," Caeden said.

I lifted Lucy into my arms, kissing the top of her tiny head. She was dressed in a cute lavender outfit with a white headband. "Daddy dressed you all fancy," I commented.

She let out a small giggle at that.

The back door opened again and our family began to pour outside. Bryce was in the lead and I couldn't cover my snicker. "Your shirt says, 'I make adorable babies,'" I shook my head.

"It's because it's true," he smirked. He held his son in front of my face. "See, Roger is said adorable baby." The poor baby was indeed wearing a onesie that said 'Adorable Baby.' Only Bryce.

Roger stuck his little tongue out at me. At six months old, Roger already acted exactly like his dad, and mostly looked like him too, except for the red hair he had inherited from Charlotte.

"Bryce! Stop waving the baby in the air like that, you're going to make him sick!" Charlotte scolded Bryce. "I swear, you're more of a pain in my butt than Roger."

"Hey, at least you don't have to change my diapers. I should get bonus points for that," Bryce smirked.

I laughed as they headed to one of the tables by the pool.

Leo and Leila, Bentley and Chris' twins, came barreling at my legs. At two years old, they were only a little younger than Grant, and absolutely adorable. They both had thick black hair like Bentley's, but their mother's pale green eyes. I could already tell that little Leo was going to be a heartbreaker one day.

"Baby?" Leila pointed up at Lucy in my arms.

"Yes, this is baby Lucy." I squatted down so the twins could see the baby.

"Pwetty," Leila patted the top of Lucy's head. "She's cuter then my dolls."

"Leila! Leo! Come over here so I can put your swim clothes on you," Christian hollered at the twins. Her stomach was already rounded with their next child—a boy they were naming Logan.

Leo was quick to run over to his mom, but Leila didn't leave.

"Is she swimmin' wif us?"

"No, sweetie," I frowned.

"Oh."

"Leila!" Chris called again.

Leila looked at Lucy one last time before running towards her mother.

Everyone else slowly trickled in. My parents, Caeden's mom, Gram, and even my old soccer buddies came with their families. They were all out of college now and had moved back here, so I tried to see them often. Caeden and I had come up with the idea to grill burgers and hotdogs once a month during the summer and have everybody over. It was our chance to all get together and hangout.

Our life had been relatively calm in the last six years—if having three kids can be thought of us as calm.

Everything in the shifter world was quiet. There was no upheaval like what we had dealt with from Travis. Everything was…peaceful.

We still didn't know what might be ahead for Beau. Neither of his siblings had been born already able to shift, and neither of my following pregnancies had been anything like my experience with Beau. Beau was special, I'd always known that, and maybe one day we'd learn just how special. Then again, maybe not. Either way, I was okay.

I grinned as I looked around at all my friends and family. My eyes lingered over Caeden, our boys, and then down at Lucy in my arms.

Life was perfect.

And they lived happily ever after...

ACKNOWLEDGEMENTS.

Writing this book was beyond emotional. Caeden and Sophie have been characters close to my heart for a very long time. I think a part of me thought their story would never end—and really it, won't. They'll live on forever in my heart and the hearts of all you readers that embraced and loved them.

Thankful doesn't even begin to describe how I feel right now. Honored, seems more correct. I'm grateful that so many of you fell in love with my characters and their story—begging for more. It's always sad to say goodbye to those characters we love so much, but I hope you've enjoyed this final installment in Caeden and Sophie's journey and feel a satisfaction in where they ended up.

I guess I better get to the *acknowledging* part and stop being sappy.

I think the biggest thanks should go to my grandma, for always supporting my dream of being an author, and encouraging me when I felt like giving up. She also deserves a round of applause for dealing with my mood swings while writing this book. Let me tell you, ending a series and knowing you have to say goodbye to characters is extremely difficult. So thank you, for always being there. I don't know what I'd do without you.

Thank you, Emily W., for always being there when I need to talk. Whether it's about the book I'm working on, or just life. You're my BFFBL and I love you!

Harper James…you're the best. That's all there is to it. Who would've thought one email would create such an amazing friendship? I don't know what I'd do if I couldn't bug you every single day! Thank you for keeping me sane and always being there for me.

Kendall McCubbin, I just love you. Seriously, you're awesome, and I'm honored to be your friend. I can't thank you enough for beta reading this book and dealing with my constant messages. I know I was a crazy person with this book, at least I feel that way, and you definitely made me feel better and helped erase my worries.

Lastly, I have to thank YOU. Yes, YOU. The one reading this. This is all for you guys. You're the reason I get to do what I love. Getting to connect with and hear from you guys always brings a smile to my face. I love y'all. I really do.

ABOUT THE AUTHOR

Micalea Smeltzer is a bestselling Young and New Adult author from Winchester, Virginia. She's always working on her next book, and when she has spare time she loves to read and spend time with her family.

Follow Micalea:
Facebook: **https://www.facebook.com/MicaleaSmeltzerfanpage?ref=hl**
Twitter: @msmeltzer9793

Instagram: micaleasmeltzer

Other Books by Micalea Smeltzer

Paranormal Romance

Fallen Series

Now Available

New Adult Contemporary Romance
Second Chances Series
Now Available

Trace + Olivia Series
Now Available

Coming Spring 2014

Standalone Adult Contemporary Romance
Now Available

Made in the USA
San Bernardino, CA
12 May 2016